Cherry Red

Cherry Red

Neil B. Hampson, MD

BEST
PUBLISHING
COMPANY

Best Publishing Company
631 US Highway 1, Suite 307
North Palm Beach, FL 33408

Front Cover Photo © Hillary DeBeer | Dreamstime.com
Back Cover Author Photo: Rick Dahms

ISBN: 978-1-9305-3693-7
ISBN: 978-1-9305-3694-4 (ebook)

Library of Congress Control Number: 2016938682

First Edition

Printed in the United States of America

This book is dedicated to Diane, Lindsay, and Courtney in appreciation of their love and support.

Chapter 1

"Intubated cherry is inbound from a hospital in the north end for emergent treatment in the chamber. Transport reportedly just left their emergency room with an ETA of twenty minutes."

Dr. Bradley Franklin had just settled down before the desktop computer monitor in his windowless Metropolitan Hospital office. Randy Johannson, one of the hyperbaric chamber operators, stood in the half-opened door awaiting the physician's instructions.

Brad put his plans on hold for catching up with overnight e-mail. In his job, he needed extreme flexibility, as emergency patients were added to his fully booked schedule on a regular basis. He noted the small clock in the corner of his computer screen read 8:05 a.m., the peak of Seattle's accurately publicized rush-hour traffic.

"Randy, that would be a world record. Go ahead and get the routine 8:30 a.m. hyperbaric treatment started, and we'll deal with it when we they get here. Will you ask Patti to give the referring emergency department a call and get the straight facts?"

He understood Randy's brief comments meant a critically ill patient with carbon monoxide poisoning would be arriving for hyperbaric oxygen treatment in an hour or so. He also knew third- or fourth-hand accounts in medicine have a tendency to be inaccurate.

A "cherry" was department slang for a patient with carbon monoxide poisoning, a term used by the staff in part to tease Brad. Carbon monoxide is a colorless, odorless, tasteless gas produced in variable amounts by combustion. Most of it comes from internal combustion engines in motor vehicles, but burning of carbon-based fuel of any kind produces carbon monoxide to some degree. Because it is invisible and can't be smelled, people can breathe carbon monoxide and not be aware of it until it poisons them.

When the poisoning victim breathes in carbon monoxide, it passes from the lungs to the bloodstream, where it binds to red blood cells and prevents them from carrying oxygen to the body tissues. It has been known since the mid-1800s that carbon monoxide turns blood a brighter color of red, classically referred to as a "cherry red."

Almost all medical textbooks say those suffering from carbon monoxide poisoning have cherry red lips and skin. This frustrated Brad. He knew having enough carbon monoxide in the blood to change one's skin color required a level so high it would be impossible to survive.

As medical director of the hyperbaric facility, he had treated over 700 cases of carbon monoxide poisoning in Metropolitan Hospital's hyperbaric oxygen chamber over the years and had never seen one patient cherry red. He had even published an article in a major medical journal trying to logically dispel the concept. However, most people in medicine, especially first responders like paramedics and emergency medicine physicians, still believed the myth.

Brad steeled himself for another busy day, and then returned to a rapid review of his inbox and the forty-seven new e-mails that had come in overnight. He knew the patient would not arrive in twenty minutes as advertised. Emergency patients were never on time.

Chapter 2

The clinical staff working the morning shift in the department gathered around Patti Silvers, the day's charge nurse, for a summary of their incoming patient.

"She is a single, twenty-three-year-old white female named Laurie Rodgers, found just after 7:00 a.m. today, unconscious in her garage, slumped over the wheel of her car with the engine running. She was intubated by medics at the scene and transported on oxygen to the nearest hospital emergency department. Workup there was notable for a blood carbon monoxide level of 43% and a negative toxicology screen for illicit drugs. The ER physician on duty thought she looked cherry red, probably after he knew the results of the labs. Chest x-ray clear, vital signs stable. Transfer was accepted by our emergency department physician."

Brad processed the information. "Do we know any more about the circumstances? Any clues as to whether this was accidental or intentional?"

"The fire department medics who picked her up thought it looked like a suicide attempt. The hillside condo where she lives in Magnolia has garages on the ground level, with housing units built above them. Each individual garage has its own door and an entrance door from the outside. The property manager for her complex was taking his morning stroll around the grounds about 7:00 a.m. He saw her enter her garage, and then heard her car horn blare continuously two or three minutes later.

"He has a master key to the garages and opened the door. When he peeked inside, he saw her slumped over the steering wheel and thought she was dead. He was afraid to go near her. He called 9-1-1 and opened the big garage door while he waited for Medic-1. They were onsite in three minutes."

"Suicide note?"

Pattie continued. "I don't know. The medics are bringing all the papers they found in the garage. If you can believe it, she is single and drives a new Cadillac Escalade. I can't believe anyone in Seattle drives one of those things. They only get about fifteen miles per gallon. Obviously not every resident of this city is interested in the environment."

Claude Fontaine, the hyperbaric engineer interrupted. "I think those Escalades are great rigs! They have a huge V-8 engine and are big enough for eight people. Do you know if it is the Platinum version? They run about ninety grand. This chick must be loaded!"

Brad ignored him and shook his head. "I don't understand it either, Patti. But remember, you guys. This woman is our patient, and we are going to take care of her the best way we can. Forget your biases against her personal choices. They have no relevance here. And Claude, act a little professional for once!"

Chapter 3

Three medics rolled noisily through the facility's back-door emergency entrance. They pushed a bright yellow steel transport stretcher while one of them bagged the comatose rider, regularly squeezing a clear resuscitation bag connected to the plastic tube inserted into her windpipe. As emergency patients were not an uncommon occurrence in the department, the hyperbaric staff greeted the medics by their first names and offered them some department coffee. Living in Seattle, all of them were devotees of good coffee, and the ambulance company they worked for was notorious for trying to keep its night shift crews awake by providing them one of the bland national brands sold in a three-pound can.

Seattle is well-known for coffee. Its residents drink more coffee per capita than anywhere else in the country. Starbucks was founded in Seattle in 1971 near the Seattle waterfront, initially just to sell coffee beans for home brewing. It eventually added espresso and other coffee and non-coffee drinks to its menu and grew worldwide. Anyone aware of the heritage of coffee in Seattle would never go near the canned stuff. The ambulance crews throughout the city always anticipated a good cup of dark roast when they came to Metro Hyperbaric. Brad saw it as a small expense for maintaining good relations with the people who transported their sickest patients.

As per his irrepressible nature, Claude tried to tease the arriving paramedics a little. "We were told you'd left St. Elsewhere at 8:00 and would be here by 8:20. It's 9:15 now. What happened? Were your lights and siren broken?"

The team leader was a statuesque woman about thirty years old, her dark brown hair pulled through the back of her baseball-style company cap in a shoulder-length ponytail. Her blue polyester jumpsuit was tight-fitting and accentuated the fullness of her bust. She responded for the group.

"Oh, you guys know how it really is, if anyone does. We didn't actually get out of the emergency department and on the road until 8:30 and the traffic on I-5 was terrible. Cars and trucks were backed up bumper-to-bumper heading southbound due to an accident under the Convention Center. Even with lights and siren, making headway is difficult in those situations. Why don't you guys move somewhere that's easier to get to than Pill Hill?"

"We're not going anywhere and leaving this state-of-the-art facility."

"It's easy to be state-of-the-art when you're the only show in town."

Brad heard the flirtatious bickering and walked over to them. "Knock it off, you two. Let's put the patient first. And that means everyone here. Now, what do you three newcomers know about this woman?"

The paramedic rig driver spoke up. "Dr. Franklin, her next-door neighbor was at the other hospital, and we talked to her in the emergency department waiting room while they prepped the patient for transport. She said the patient works as a receptionist at a downtown law firm just so she has something to do. Doesn't need the income because she apparently inherited a bunch of money. Her new Escalade has a custom paint job in the Seahawks football team's colors—navy, green, and gray."

"Does she have any known medical problems?"

"Not that the neighbor knew of, and they are apparently pretty close."

"Medications?"

"Nope."

"History of depression, previous suicide attempts, recent life stresses?"

"Not really. As I said, the neighbor knows her well and says she seems to lead a charmed life, just doing whatever she wants. She broke up with her latest boyfriend about a week ago, but that's apparently nothing unusual for her. The only new thing is this huge SUV she bought a month ago. She can hardly fit it in her garage. She told the neighbor it was running a little rough after she was at Green Lake Sunday morning. It apparently ran fine on the way there but acted up after she parked and went for a run around the lake. Certainly nothing that would cause someone to try to off themselves."

By the time she had finished answering his questions, Brad had completed a brief examination of the patient. The only remarkable findings were her intubation with an endotracheal tube for ventilation, comatose state, regular vital signs, clear lungs with equal breath sounds, and the absence of cherry red coloration of her skin or lips.

The physician then opened a document on a computer monitor at the nurses' station. It automatically populated with the names of the department staff on duty in different positions that day from the online staff schedule. "Okay, team, let's run the critical care checklist we put together to make sure we don't miss anything and thereby hurt the patient. We all have a job. Charge nurse, Patti Silvers . . . Does she have an arterial line for sampling blood gases at depth so we can adjust her ventilator?"

She nodded. "Yes. Put in at the local hospital and functioning well on a pressure bag here. The wave form looks great on the monitor, and it draws blood easily."

"Respiratory therapy, Rick? Is the ventilator calibrated?"

Rick Blodgett had come down from the Critical Care Unit (CCU) when he was paged and quietly entered the chamber room during the preceding activity. "Yep. Ready to go, Boss. I calibrated on an estimated weight of fifty-five kilograms."

Brad glanced at the patient and roughly estimated her

weight. "That seems about right. We can fine-tune when we get the first blood gases back. Next on the checklist, managing physician to review chest x-ray. That's my responsibility. I had them repeat one on her during transit through our emergency department to check endotracheal tube position after transport. I already looked at the x-ray on the computer monitor. The ventilation tube is in good position. Lung fields were clear, no sign of aspiration or collapsed lung."

Brad continued reading from the computer. "Last on the intubated carbon monoxide checklist, Hyperbaric Engineer Claude Fontaine, replace air in the endotracheal tube cuff with saline."

No one replied.

Brad repeated, "Fill ETT cuff with saline."

When there was again no reply, he looked up to see Claude across the room with the attractive female paramedic who had accompanied the patient. They were looking at the department's saltwater aquarium.

"Claude, this task is yours. Did you do it?"

Claude stopped pointing at the geoduck clam in the aquarium. "What task, Brad?"

"Fill the cuff with saline. Obviously you didn't. Rick, will you take care of it so we can get going? It's 9:40 a.m. We'll start her treatment in the entry lock, then move her across to Treatment Lock 1 when the six folks in the routine 8:30 a.m. treatment get out at 10:30."

The forty-eight-foot-long cylindrical steel chamber had been divided into three compartments or locks, all equipped with doors on each end for this type of emergency flexibility.

"We'll treat on the US Air Force Carbon Monoxide Table, maximum pressure three atmospheres absolute or sixty-six feet of seawater depth equivalent. Remember, our goal is to prevent persistent or delayed brain injury. Let's compress, people."

Brad was irritated with the lack of attention Claude had exhibited when dealing with a critically ill patient and wanted the staff to know it. "And at our next quarterly staff meeting, Claude will be giving us a presentation on how checklists in medicine save lives."

Chapter 4

A mechanical respirator mounted on the wall of the chamber's central entry lock was ventilating the unconscious patient. Critical care nurse Dawna Harris stepped inside and used both hands to push the heavy two-inch-thick steel door closed. Dawna was off that day from her usual job in the critical care unit at Bellevue Hospital on the east side of Lake Washington. She worked per-diem for Metro's Hyperbaric Department and took emergency calls about three shifts a month. While others had been setting up for the treatment, she had driven from home after her pager alarmed.

Randy operated the chamber from the console. He pulled his headset microphone down in front of his mouth. "Ready to go, Dawna?"

"All set, " she replied through her wireless headset.

Randy set the maximum depth for the treatment at sixty-six feet of seawater pressure, the pressurization rate at ten feet per minute, and pushed the button to start the chamber compression. Under the department floor were two huge volume tanks filled with pressurized air that slowly bled into the chamber. Six compressors in another room had filled the volume tanks previously. Because recently compressed gas is hot, air straight from the compressors could not be vented into the chambers. Instead, the volume tanks were filled and the pressurized air allowed to cool before being used.

Inside the chamber, Dawna stood next to the patient's stretcher. A faint hissing noise indicated pressurized air entered the chamber. As the chamber pressurized, the air within it warmed, and Dawna broke out in a light sweat. Every so often, she used the Valsalva maneuver to adjust her middle ear pressure to equal the pressure inside the chamber. She pinched her nose, held her breath, and bore down as if blowing up a balloon.

Brad also wore one of the wireless communication headsets outside the chamber because he liked to stay in contact with the inside attendant during the compression of a critically ill patient. "We're passing thirty feet, Dawna. How's the patient?"

"She's starting to grimace like she is in discomfort. She's probably having ear squeeze."

Brad looked at the scene inside the chamber on the console video monitor. "I agree with you. It's hard to clear your ears with an endotracheal tube in place. Let's give her some intravenous fentanyl for the discomfort. It's actually a good thing she is starting to respond to pain. Maybe she'll wake up. I want to minimize sedation during the treatment as long as she remains cooperative."

Randy interrupted. "Just reached treatment pressure of sixty-six feet. I'm switching the patient's breathing manifold to 100% oxygen. Dawna, I know it's pretty warm in the small entry lock after chamber compression to three atmospheres. I'll ventilate some air from the volume tanks through the lock to cool it down initially, and the water-based air conditioning system will keep you comfortable from that point on."

Brad reviewed the printed treatment protocol attached to the console clipboard in front of Randy, even though he could recite every detail of it from memory due to his extensive prior experience. "We've got two twenty-three-minute oxygen breathing periods at sixty-six feet, then we slide to thirty-three feet for two twenty-five-minute periods. Please draw blood gases from the arterial line five minutes before the end of the first oxygen period so we can fine tune the ventilator. Since everything looks stable at this point, I'll be down the hall in my office. Give me a buzz when you have the lab results back."

Brad took off the headset and laid it on the counter. As he walked back to his office, he thought about the terrific team he had assembled, among the best in the country. Every one of them was nationally certified for their position by the Hyperbaric Medical Society. He had total confidence in them and felt he could trust each of them completely, even Claude. They worked as a team exceptionally well. He encouraged a first-name basis for all of his staff so they felt equal. In doing so, he could be certain someone would speak up when they had an idea or noticed something being done improperly or in a manner dangerous for patients. Staff suggestions were implemented regularly and the department's safety record impeccable.

Chapter 5

Like most subspecialty physicians, the forty-eight-year-old Brad had paid his dues by training at a variety of locations around the country. There is an unwritten philosophy in medical circles: being educated in several different medical centers makes a physician more well-rounded and gives him or her better perspective in patient care because the art of medicine is practiced differently around the country. Accordingly, he completed his four years of medical school at the University of Washington in Seattle, a three-year internal medicine residency at the University of Minnesota, and then three years of Pulmonary and Critical Care Fellowship at Duke University in North Carolina. He had gotten his card punched at all the appropriate stops along the way.

Brad learned hyperbaric medicine during his fellowship at Duke. Because of their role as one of the country's leading research universities, it is not surprising their hyperbaric chamber complex is one of the nation's largest. Duke had eight steel chambers of varying size and configuration, used to pressurize and administer oxygen to patients and experimental subjects.

Hyperbaric oxygen therapy was just beginning to gain a foothold of legitimacy within modern medicine when Brad trained at Duke. Most people had heard of hyperbaric chambers because some of the emergent conditions treated tended to be newsworthy: divers with decompression sickness (the bends), families with carbon monoxide poisoning, or people with severe infections like gas gangrene.

While the stories of these patients frequently found their way into the lay media, the emergent patients typically received only one or a few treatments. Not many in the public realized hyperbaric oxygen was also used to treat chronic conditions such as non-healing leg wounds from diabetes or tissue broken down from radiation therapy for cancer. Since these non-emergent patients received an average of thirty to forty daily two-hour hyperbaric treatments, they really made up the bulk of the facility's treatment volume.

The Silent Majority.

Chapter 6

B rad had returned to Seattle after finishing his medical training for several reasons. His Midwest and East Coast colleagues were incredulous when he told them one of the reasons was the weather. It always entertained him how effectively a campaign of disinformation was once spread nationally by a Seattle newspaper editorialist, in essence preventing a wave of migration by Californians fleeing overcrowding and ridiculous home prices in the 1980s.

Anyone who has not lived in Seattle seems to tell Brad it rains all the time there. He was somewhat smug when he told them Seattle has an annual precipitation of about thirty-eight inches, less than most major East Coast cities, including New York, Atlanta, and Miami.

He was also attracted back to the Northwest by the city of Seattle itself. Seattle is built on several hills, some of the prominent ones being First Hill (also known as Pill Hill because of the many hospitals located there),

Beacon Hill, Queene Anne Hill, Capitol Hill, and Magnolia. He lived with his wife and two daughters in a quiet, family-focused neighborhood on Queene Anne and walked to work at Metropolitan Hospital in about thirty-five minutes, cutting through the heart of the city.

As he walked, he had intermittent views of Elliott Bay between the downtown buildings. Brad could smell the salty sea air and hear the rumbling horns of the ferries that shuttle commuters and their cars back and forth across the chilly Puget Sound waters, even though his usual route kept him several blocks from the waterfront. Thursday mornings were administrative for Brad, allowing him the extra time to detour through the Pike Place Market for fresh-baked croissants or a slice of quiche Lorraine at the French bakery. He always smiled at the tourists taking selfies in front of what is known as the original Starbucks. Only natives remember the first Starbucks was on Western Avenue, relocated in 1976 to the Market where it remains today.

The natural beauty of the region and availability of outdoor recreational activities in all four seasons of the year also appealed to Brad. Even though it could be overcast and drizzly on a Saturday in January, the daytime temperature is in the forties or fifties, allowing residents to don their rain gear and go hiking in the foothills of the Cascade Mountains or sailing in Puget Sound.

But most of all, it was the people that had attracted him back to Seattle. Almost no one living in the city is a native: you rarely met someone who was born there. Most have emigrated from other parts of the country because of the climate, the metropolitan opportunities offered by the city counterbalanced by the outdoor activities offered by nature, and also to live in an area populated by people similar to themselves.

In contrast to most major US cities, a large proportion of Seattle's population is green—interested in the environment and the pursuit of activities at both individual and community levels to help preserve the Earth. In Seattle, the hybrid and all-electric cars introduced in recent years were extremely popular among those who did not walk, bike, or take the bus to work. No-cost citywide curbside recycling had reduced the garbage flow into landfills by over 50%, and the population seemed to recognize the need to respect the environment in general. As Brad was a true native, having been born in the city and grown up in a Seattle suburb, he appreciated being surrounded by people wanting to help maintain an area of the country he considered selfishly his own.

Since coming to Metro fifteen years earlier, his practice had flourished. Raising patients' blood oxygen levels as high as possible by having them breathe pure oxygen in a pressurized chamber seemed to integrate well with his feelings about the environment. It was a natural therapy.

Of the fourteen conditions approved for treatment with hyperbaric oxygen in the United States, Brad's area of special interest and expertise was carbon monoxide poisoning. Because his department treated sixty to one hundred severe cases in the hyperbaric chamber at

Metro each year, there was ample opportunity for clinical research about the condition.

As a result of his academic involvement with carbon monoxide poisoning, the hyperbaric nurses and technicians at Metro were relative experts, too. If they expressed interest, Brad recruited them to work on a research project, often involving a search through the old medical records of previously treated patients looking for some small tidbit of a clue explaining why or how their form of carbon monoxide poisoning occurred or could be prevented.

Even if a staff member did not have an interest in research, they could not avoid learning about carbon monoxide poisoning. Brad lectured to the staff on the topic regularly, especially emphasizing the new research findings produced in their own department. Such involvement engendered tremendous staff pride in their department's national reputation.

Chapter 7

After being called to return to the chamber room, Brad sat at the ten-foot-long counter constituting the department's nursing station. He read the laboratory results now available on the computer monitor aloud to his team.

"The blood gases look good. Arterial pH is 7.31, carbon dioxide 32 and oxygen level greater than 760. Rick, there is no need to adjust the ventilator. Carbon dioxide is a little low, but it is compensating for the metabolic acidosis related to her carbon monoxide poisoning."

"Okay. She is actually lightening up already and triggering the ventilator herself."

"That's great. An early response to the hyperbaric oxygen treatment suggests a better outcome. As long as we are on the topic of mechanical ventilation in the hyperbaric environment, can you explain to the group why the checklist indicated saline needed to replace the air in her endotracheal tube cuff prior to treatment?"

"Because the air in the cuff will get compressed during chamber pressurization?"

"Right. And when the balloon-like cuff is essentially squished flat, what will happen?"

"An air leak around the tube will be present."

"Why is that bad?"

"Because we are using positive pressure ventilation to drive breathing gas into the lungs, and our ability to ventilate the patient would be impaired."

"Do we need to ventilate this particular patient more or less than usual?"

"She is being ventilated about 25% more than normal to make up for her metabolic acidosis."

Brad smiled because Rick understood the concept perfectly. "Exactly right. And without the ability to effectively ventilate her, a respiratory acidosis could compound her metabolic problem and make her blood pH even lower. This could potentially result in cardiac rhythm disturbances and even death. This has been a good lesson for Claude, and the rest of you should remember it, as well. Your task on the checklist is important, and it is there for a reason. Forgetting something could determine life or death for a patient. We use checklists for the same reason airline pilots do."

After two oxygen-breathing periods at sixty-six feet of seawater pressure, the chamber was slowly decompressed to thirty-three feet of seawater for administration of two additional twenty-five-minute oxygen periods. A few minutes after decompression started, Dawna's voice crackled over the headsets worn by the chamber operator and charge nurse. "Hey, you guys. Zoom in on the patient's face on your monitor."

Randy flipped a switch on the console, and the image on the chamber monitor changed from a view of the entire chamber interior to the patient from the chest up, lying on the stretcher. Other than the presence of the plastic tube going through her mouth into her windpipe, she looked remarkably normal. Her eyes were open and tracking Dawna as she moved about the chamber. The patient could be seen trying to talk, and then realize something prevented it. Her hands came up to her face and explored the endotracheal tube. Dawna gently moved her hands away from the tube to keep her from unintentionally pulling it out.

"Laurie, you're okay. You breathed in some carbon monoxide from your car exhaust, and it made you sick. You are in the hyperbaric chamber at Metropolitan Hospital where we are giving you lots of oxygen to wash the carbon monoxide out of your system. That tube goes into your lungs, and it is hooked up to a machine called a ventilator that breathes for you. We're almost done."

Laurie nodded and laid her arms at her side.

Dawna looked straight into the camera. "We've got another save, guys. We do good work, don't we?"

Chapter 8

Exactly two hours and fifteen minutes after the big steel door closed, it cracked open with a hiss around the edges as the last of the pressurized air was released. The stretcher that had carried the previously critically ill patient into the chamber was rolled out and into the nearby treatment room.

Brad and Patti assumed positions on either side of the stretcher. "Laurie, I'm Dr. Bradley Franklin, medical director of this department, and this is Patti Silvers, one of our nurses. How do you feel?"

Unable to talk due to the tube, the patient shrugged her shoulders, then brightened and gave him the thumbs-up sign.

"That's great. You did very well in the hyperbaric chamber. We'll be sending you up to the Critical Care Unit where you'll be seen and evaluated by some other physicians. I'm sure one of their top priorities will be to get that tube out. They'll have you do some simple tests to insure you can breathe on your own first. I'll stop by to see you before I go home this evening."

Laurie nodded in understanding and reached out both hands to grasp Brad's hand resting on the stretcher railing. She mouthed the words, "Thank you."

Brad looked down at the patient and smiled. "You're welcome. It is our pleasure to help you."

He then redirected his attention to Patti across the stretcher. "Please call the CCU and give them the patient's information. Then call inpatient transport and let them know we've got an intubated patient on a stretcher needing to go to the CCU. I'll call the house staff and tell them about their admission."

"Got it. By the way, there is some fantastic home-made strawberry-rhubarb pie in the breakroom, made by the wife of one of the patients in the 8:30 treatment. It tastes great with good coffee."

"I guess I know what I'm having for lunch. Thanks for your help this morning."

His staff knew he enjoyed quality coffee. It was difficult to avoid when living in a city where there are estimated to be over 400 Starbucks stores. In some Starbucks locations, it is possible to sit in a comfortable lounge chair enjoying a beverage and look across or down the street and see another Starbucks.

As he walked back to his office thinking about an early lunch, Brad reminded himself to ask the admitting CCU resident to request a consultation from the psychiatry service once the patient was extubated, off the ventilator, and able to talk. As it was possible this poisoning may have been intentional, Laurie would need to be evaluated for ongoing risk of self-harm prior to discharge.

Chapter 9

Dr. Charles James, a nationally recognized expert in the management of chronic wounds and also board-certified in hyperbaric medicine, occupied the office next to Brad's. Charles had a second office in Metropolitan's Wound Healing Center, a facility elsewhere in the medical center that drew patient referrals from across the country because of his reputation.

This was typical of the six hyperbaric physicians supervised by Brad at Metropolitan. Each worked part-time in hyperbaric medicine and practiced in another specialty part-time. Brad believed this was important for the cross fertilization of new ideas to be incorporated into hyperbaric medicine. Also, each practiced with a different style, and he felt this variety was good for his staff. Exposing them to different viewpoints stimulated them to think and learn, similar to the concept of doing medical training across the country.

As he walked by the open door, Brad noticed Charles was at his desk looking at wound photographs on his two giant thirty-two inch desktop computer monitors. "You just can't get enough of that stuff, can you?"

Charles looked up. "Oh, hi Brad. I was just preparing some images for a presentation I am giving this coming weekend in London."

"Tough duty. Are you working today?"

"Yeah, I was in the Wound Center all morning and am covering hyperbaric this afternoon. Anything interesting?"

"We had a strange carbon monoxide case. A wealthy young woman apparently attempted suicide by running her vehicle in a closed garage. She was found unconscious in the driver's seat of her new SUV. The strange thing is, if you believe the story of the property manager who discovered her and called it in, she was only in there for a couple of minutes before losing consciousness."

"You're the expert on carbon monoxide poisoning, but that doesn't sound unusual to me. What bothers you?"

"Two things. First, the timing doesn't fit. She could not have been running her car long enough for the carbon monoxide in the garage to build up to the kind of level she must have been exposed to. Second, the reason she would attempt suicide is not at all obvious. Things had been going well for her. She apparently had the world by the tail."

"Maybe the manager was wrong about how long she was in the garage. Or maybe something was wrong with her car, and it was putting out more carbon monoxide than you'd expect it to. Or *maybe* it wasn't suicide but murder! Any chance this manager guy held a grudge for some reason and kindly started her car for her a couple of hours earlier?"

"Chuck, you are always so melodramatic. I don't know the answers to your questions because I haven't talked to her yet. I'm going to try to see her after she is extubated. I'll let you know how things turn out when you get back from your trip. Have fun in London and bring me back a box of Bendick's Bittermints from duty-free at Heathrow. I love those things."

Brad continued down the hall, thinking about Laurie Rodgers as he walked.

Chapter 10

Brad put the last piece of completed paperwork for the day in the out-basket on his desk and left the Hyperbaric Department, headed for the CCU. As he walked the nearly empty late-afternoon halls of the medical center to the next pavilion, it struck him hospitals always grew laterally, not vertically.

In every medical center in which he had worked, expansion occurred by constructing a new building or pavilion and attaching it to the existing complex. The end result was often a historical tour of architecture as one walked from one end to the other and a complex maze for the unfamiliar visitor.

He also realized the most acute care was typically moved to the new state-of-the-art building. Other departments with less critically ill patients gradually moved upstream in turn. As he entered Metropolitan's ultra-modern CCU, it struck him as ironic that medical center administration often was relegated to the oldest part of the complex. His own department's administrator, Taylor Marks, was one of the vice presidents in the institution. He held an advanced business degree from Harvard and was bright. But he watched the numbers from the Hyperbaric Department so closely, he often showed up in Brad's office wanting to discuss new budget performance data before he had even received any reports. It did not disappoint Brad that Taylor had an office with the rest of the administration in the oldest wing, far from the Hyperbaric Medicine Department. The patient comes first, as they should, he thought to himself.

"Hi, Pam. Can you tell me what bed Laurie Rodgers is in and where I can find the CCU resident?"

Pam Olsen had been a unit clerk in Metropolitan's CCU as long as Brad could remember. She always worked the weekday swing shift, and since he usually visited patients in the unit at the end of his workday, it seemed she was always there. Even though she was probably approaching fifty, Brad thought she still looked thirty-five. She had naturally blond hair typical of the Scandinavians who had once immigrated in droves to Seattle because of the similarity of the geography and climate to their homeland. Her skin was almost milky-white, typical of someone who had not intentionally sought a suntan throughout her life. Combined with a slim figure toned by hours on the cross-trainer every week, it seemed to Brad she looked no older than she did when he came to Metro fifteen years earlier.

"Hi Brad," she said, smiling and adopting the first name familiarity Brad encouraged among his hyperbaric staff and feeling justified because they had known each other so long. "The patient is in room six. I saw the resident, Dr. David Marklin, just carry his cafeteria dinner tray into the conference room to eat, if you are looking for him."

Dave was a third-year internal medicine resident from Missouri who was very sharp and equally confident in his abilities. Like other upper-level residents who know they are good, he was a little cocky.

"Hi, Dr. Franklin," he said, looking up from the stuffed baked potato on his plate but showing no intention of postponing his meal when the senior physician entered the room. "I'll bet you are looking for the patient with carbon monoxide poisoning."

"You're right. How is she doing?"

"When she hit the unit at noon, it seemed she was quite awake. We held all sedation and gave her a spontaneous breathing trial. She passed, and I had her extubated by one o'clock. She's in room six watching television right now, only on two liters oxygen per minute. I'll probably send her out to a floor bed this evening."

"Did someone from psychiatry see her?"

"Yeah, they weren't much help. All they could say was she denies any current intent to harm herself and she could be discharged when medically stable."

"What did she tell you about the event? Was this an intentional exposure? Did she start the car herself or was it running when she walked into the garage?"

"Million-dollar question, Dr. F. She doesn't remember much of anything for the past twenty-four hours, including why she was passed out in the garage in a running car. My bet is she did it to get attention from someone."

"It's certainly possible, but people making such a gesture usually leave a note to the person whose attention they seek. The medics brought all the papers in her car, and no suicide note was found. I think I'll go talk to her myself now that she is extubated."

Brad walked across the unit to room CCU-6, pulled the door curtain aside, and walked in. Laurie was sitting up in her hospital bed, wearing a clean gown, eating a bowl of chicken broth, and watching a rerun of *Star Trek* on the blaring television mounted up in the corner of the room.

"Hi, Laurie. Remember me? I'm Dr. Franklin from the Hyperbaric Department. We treated you this morning in the chamber. Can we turn the TV down and talk for a few minutes?"

"Yes, I remember seeing you this morning. I just can't remember things before the treatment. It's like I have a defective sector on my hard drive. The last thing I remember before waking up in your hyperbaric chamber is driving home last night. I went clubbing after work and came home about twelve-thirty. I remember the drive because I had to stop to fill up my gas tank on the way home and it was hard to find an open station."

"I heard your car has been running a little rough lately."

"Yeah, I drove to Green Lake Sunday morning for a run. When I got done, my car wouldn't start because I was out of gas. The fuel light was on when I drove there, but I thought I'd have enough to get by. When I didn't, this guy hanging around the parking lot said he would sell me some from a gas container for his lawnmower in the back of his pickup truck. He ripped me off for twenty bucks for two gallons! He said it was a delivery fee. I didn't have any cash with me so I wrote him a check. And then something was wrong with the gas because my car coughed and sputtered for the past two days. It ran out last night. That's why I stopped to fill up."

"Sounds like the gas may have been old or had some water in it. Anyway, have you been depressed lately or had thoughts about harming yourself?"

"No, why would I? My life is great. I've got everything I want."

"Ever had depression in the past?"

"No. No one in the Rodgers family has ever seen a shrink."

"Tell me about this morning."

"Like I've told you and everyone else already, I don't remember anything for about eight or ten hours. How many times do I have to repeat myself? Listen, I want to get out of here. There is this guy I met last night at the new club in Belltown. I want to go back and see if he is there again tonight. Can you get me discharged?"

"You obviously remember last evening. Sorry, but I'm going to recommend they keep you overnight because of your short-term memory loss. Memory problems are common after carbon monoxide poisoning. You may never recall the events right around the poisoning, but otherwise you should do well."

"What makes you think you have the power to keep me in this place? I know my rights. I work in a law firm, you know!"

"Yes, I am aware of that. But it would be to your advantage to cooperate with me. Remember, you may have attempted suicide and I can call County Mental Health and ask them to have you evaluated for admission to the locked ward in County Hospital for observation."

Laurie fumed but knew being transferred to a locked psychiatric ward at County was the last thing she wanted. "Okay, you win this time. I'll stay one night."

Brad walked out of her room, justifying in his mind the white lie he had just told. County Mental Health was unlikely to commit her since Metro psychiatry had said she was no longer suicidal. But overnight observation was not unreasonable in light of her memory loss.

He took the stairs to the first floor and walked out the front entrance of Metropolitan Hospital, enjoying the early August evening. As is typical of Seattle in the summer, the temperature was seventy-two degrees, skies clear, and no rain for three weeks. He thought the nature of Seattle summers was as unknown to those living outside the Pacific Northwest as the nature of Seattle winters was publicized. It rarely rained from July through September, few homes were air conditioned due to moderate temperatures, and you could eat dinner outdoors on your deck every evening without being bothered by insects.

Despite the pleasant evening and clear skies, his mind was clouded by the circumstances of patient Laurie Rodgers. Something didn't fit.

Chapter 11

Walking into the Hyperbaric Medicine Department the following morning, Brad spotted Claude, the hyperbaric engineer, setting up the chamber for the 8:30 a.m. treatment, often called a "dive" since the chamber pressurization simulates the effects of going underwater.

"Morning, Claude. Any activity overnight? I didn't get any calls."

Claude looked up from his daily safety inspection of the acrylic viewports of the giant steel chamber, a cylinder the size of a Boeing 737 jet aircraft. "Hey. No, it was quiet. The diver the Coast Guard reported missing offshore near Port Angeles turned out to be a prank. After getting to depth, he apparently swam away from his buddy, followed the bottom to shore, and left the scene. He was recognized in a bar in Sequim when they showed his picture on the television news. I'll bet that's the last time the buddy dives with the jerk."

Brad looked up from the black plastic clipboard holding a paper printout of the weekly patient treatment schedule. "Yeah, probably. But both were responsible. You're not supposed to lose sight of your dive buddy in the first place. Diving would be so much safer if we could just convince everyone to follow the basic safety rules they were taught in training."

"How well I know." Like many working in the field of hyperbaric medicine, Claude was a scuba diving enthusiast. Before taking the job as Metropolitan Hospital's hyperbaric engineer in his mid-thirties, he had spent twelve years as a diver for the US Navy, stationed last at the Keyport Dive Locker located just across Puget Sound from Seattle. He was now a certified recreational scuba instructor and took Wednesdays off from his job at Metro to work part-time giving lessons for one of the local dive shops.

One-half of the two-car garage at his modest home was named Claude's Corner, where he ran a small business buying and reselling used dive gear and providing other minor services to scuba divers. He had an old four-teen-foot Livingston, a two-hulled fiberglass boat with a thirty-five horsepower outboard motor on a trailer he occasionally used to take undiscriminating divers on day-long dive trips on Puget Sound. Like many ex-Navy divers, he was notoriously single.

Patti had walked into the chamber area during the discussion of the formerly missing diver. She shook her head knowingly. She was married to a former commercial diver from Louisiana.

"Hi, guys. Nice weather, huh?" she asked with a slight southern drawl.

Brad set the clipboard down on the counter. "Good morning. What's today's routine schedule look like?"

"You'll be happy. We have four six-packs."

She used department jargon to describe four scheduled two-hour chamber runs, each with six patients.

"I guess Donald would say that makes a full case, huh?"

Her comment about her husband made Brad smile.

"Divers party too much."

As he strolled to his office at the other end of the department, he realized Patti was right. He was happy. The department's budget for the year was predicated on treating eighteen patients a day, and it was always better to be ahead of budget rather than behind when you deal with hospital administrators—especially when you had one who watched the numbers as closely as Taylor Marks.

Chapter 12

B rad supervised the initiation of the routine 8:30 a.m. treatment, ensuring that all the patients within the steel chamber were able to clear their ears and successfully reach the treatment pressure. Once they had donned their clear oxygen delivery hoods with assistance from the inside attendant and relaxed in the big recliner chairs to read or take a nap, Brad went to his office to make a private phone call. He looked up the number on his cell phone, but then used his desk phone to place the call because cell reception was lousy within the hospital.

"This is Detective Heimbigner. How can I help you?"

"Hi, Bob. This is Brad Franklin. How are you?"

"Oh, hi Brad. I'm fine. At least it's not raining. What's up?"

Brad and Bob had been roommates during their freshman year at the University of Washington almost three decades earlier. He chuckled when he heard Bob's comment about the weather. Bob had grown up in eastern Washington State, in the town of Yakima. Yakima, classified as a desert, is located in the rain shadow of the Cascade Mountain range. When moisture-laden clouds are pushed inland off the Pacific Ocean by the jet stream, they have to rise to clear the Cascade Range. As they rise, cooling occurs which results in condensation and rain in western Washington but not eastern Washington. Yakima only gets about seven inches of rain a year.

Even though Bob had stayed in Seattle for the twenty-five years since graduating from the UW, he still complained about the weather as much as he did when they were roommates.

"Bob, it hasn't rained in almost a month."

"Yeah, that may be true, but November is only three months away and you know what that means. Did you know Yakima only gets about seven or eight inches of precipitation per year? Give me that climate any day."

"Yeah, you've told me once or twice. But I didn't call to talk about our beautiful summer weather. What are you working on these days?"

"Lately, I've been focused on shutting down chop shops."

"Chop shops?"

"Yeah, when someone steals a car, it's hard for them to move it intact because it gets recognized. So what a lot of thieves do is take the car to an old warehouse or garage and chop it into pieces, then sell those."

"Why would anyone want to buy a piece of a chopped up car?"

"Brad, you're being too literal. Always have been. What they do is disassemble the car into parts people want. If you need a new bumper for your Mercedes, it's a lot cheaper to buy one from a chop shop than the dealer."

"Oh, now I understand. Listen. I have a story I'd like to run by you. It involves a patient we treated yesterday. It may be nothing, but I'm suspicious there could be foul play involved. Can I buy you lunch today?"

"Well, I was supposed to go on a chop shop raid in the North End with my team. But I've trained them well, and I'm sure they can handle it without me. Besides, if it is the usual scenario wherein you can't leave the medical center, then we get to eat in the hospital cafeteria."

"We don't need to. I can have my secretary order some box lunches, and we can eat in our department conference room."

"Are you kidding? I'm only coming because we will eat in the cafeteria. We don't have nurses at every table in the courthouse lunchroom."

"Bob, you haven't changed, either. See you around noon."

Chapter 13

Cathy, the department's administrative assistant, stuck her head in through Brad's open office door and said, "Boss, there is some guy out here at the reception desk who not only claims to be a Seattle policeman, but also claims he was your college roommate. He doesn't have a uniform on and looks ten years older than you."

"Is he totally bald and wearing mirrored sunglasses indoors?"

"Yep."

"Really tanned?"

"Yep, looks like he just came back from Arizona."

"More likely Yakima. I know him. Bring him back. Thanks, Cathy."

Bob strolled into Brad's office. "Hey, Brad! Great to see you. It's been too long."

Brad walked out from behind his desk and embraced his old friend. "Great to see you, too. I think it's been three years. Do you mind if we talk before we go get some lunch? I don't want anyone to overhear us. By the way, are you carrying?"

"Sure we can talk here. And of course I'm carrying. I'm a detective."

"I need to ask you to unload. This is a hospital. It's a place where we take care of people who get shot."

"Okay, okay." Bob reached inside his blazer, pulled a Glock 19 from his shoulder holster, ejected the magazine and the round in the chamber, and put it in his pocket. He then pulled up his left pants leg, removed a .38 snub nose revolver from a leg holster, unlocked the cylinder, and dumped the cartridges on Brad's desk. "Happy?"

"Wow. What do you need such an arsenal for?"

"Keeping you safe, Brad. These chop shop guys don't welcome me with open arms."

Twenty minutes later, Brad finished his summarization of Laurie Rodgers's situation. "So, what do you think?"

"There are a lot of possibilities, ranging from the over-active imagination of a middle-aged doctor to attempted murder. I need to talk to the woman who was poisoned, her boss, and the property manager. I'd like to talk to the jerk from the parking lot at Green Lake who sold her gas for ten dollars a gallon, the gas station attendant, and the guy she met at the club, if I can find them. I'm going to check out the poisoning scene and her car."

"What are you thinking?"

"I don't come to conclusions until I have the facts. It will take me a week. Now, can we go to your renowned cafeteria and scope out some nurses?"

"Sure, Detective Heimbigner. It's nice to know there are some things you can always depend on."

Chapter 14

One week later to the day, Cathy pushed her head in the half-closed door of Brad's office and said, "Boss, your old roommate is back."

He looked up from his computer, not immediately grasping what she said. He was in the middle of writing a paper for a medical journal and was concentrating hard on the task. "What did you say, Cathy? Who?"

"Detective Bob."

"Oh, great. Send him in."

Bob walked into the office holding his jacket open, revealing an empty holster. "I left them in the car, Buddy. Now if something goes down in this department while I am here, your ass is grass."

"Don't worry. It won't. What did you find out?"

"Well, I started with the possibilities this was suicidal poisoning, accidental poisoning, or attempted murder. I talked to the complex manager first. The guy doesn't act like he knows much, but it is obvious he has a fixation on this woman. He knew exactly what time she goes to work, what time she gets home, and the dates of her condo and new car purchases. It's certainly possible he would want her dead because he worships her and she ignores him. He said she came out of the building that day between 7:00 and 7:05 a.m. as she usually does, went into her garage, and was in there three minutes max before the vehicle horn started blaring. I believe his times because I think he probably watches her closely.

"I had him let me into her garage while she was at work. Most interesting. There was a bunch of crap stored in there ranging from a snowboard to beach chairs to boxes of old magazines like *Cosmopolitan*. While looking around, I saw a half roll of metal duct tape sitting on top of a pile of boxes. Now this woman doesn't sound like the type who is fixing a lot of stuff with duct tape. The manager said he didn't know anything about it or what it was doing there. Then I looked at the back of the garage door and saw pieces of the same tape hanging from the doorframe. It appeared the cracks around the door had been taped from the inside recently."

Brad said, "Sounds like a suicide attempt. It is common for a person who attempts suicide in a garage with carbon monoxide from a motor vehicle to tape all the leaks and then run the vehicle in the airtight space."

"Doctor, you are jumping to conclusions again. It doesn't prove suicide, but it probably does exclude an accidental poisoning. The woman could have duct-taped the door to attempt suicide, but someone who wanted to cause her harm might have done it, too. The door lock into the garage is a simple single cylinder anyone could open with an electric lock pick in thirty seconds. Even more, this manager is a computer geek and probably a hacker. We went up to his unit to talk, and he had computers everywhere. It made me wonder whether he might be one of those guys who can hack into people's car computer systems. Lately, they have figured out how to take over complete control of a car from a laptop, and I wondered if he had remotely started her vehicle a couple of hours before she came down that morning.

"So, next I talked to her boss, Alan Todd, at the law firm where she works. A really, really, great guy. Says Ms. Rodgers is a good employee, especially since she doesn't need to work. Her parents bought fifty grand worth of Microsoft stock in 1988, and you know where it went from there. They died in a 2008 car wreck while vacationing on the North Carolina Outer Banks. Since then, the stock price increased something like seventy times. Their only child inherited millions. Alan can't imagine she would be trying to commit suicide. By the way, he and I are going to the Seahawks's preseason game against Green Bay this weekend on his firm's tickets. A great guy."

Brad shook his head knowingly. "I'm not going to ask how the topic of the Seahawks came up. So, someone was trying to kill her?"

"Probably, but I don't know who. Talking to Ms. Rodgers didn't give me a lot of insight. She claims no one would want to kill her. She did break up with this boyfriend a week before but says the desire for a split was mutual. I tried to track down the guy from Green Lake, but she can't remember any details about him. She wrote him a check for the two gallons of gas but didn't ask his name or fill in a name on the check. I called the bank, and the check hasn't cleared.

"She can't remember his vehicle make, model, or color. Just says it was a new pickup with a canopy over the bed. So what pickup on this side of the mountains does not have a canopy? Everyone has one to protect his/her load from the rain. I spent Sunday morning at Green Lake and didn't see any guys hanging out alone in the parking lot. There aren't a lot of pickup trucks there, either. You know, in eastern Washington, everyone drives a pickup. Folks recognize the value of a good half-ton. I just don't understand people on this side of the mountains. What are you driving these days?"

"Toyota Prius."

"I would have expected as much. Keep an eye on your car. Chop shops love them for their batteries. Anyway, she told me the story about meeting a guy at this Belltown club last Monday night, too. She had been there a few times since but has never seen him again. I even went with her to the club this Monday night, and she couldn't ID him. It wasn't a wasted trip, though. I nailed one of the chop kings I've been looking for in the men's room there, and then had the place shut down for serving minors. Speaking of that, remember when we had fake

IDs to go out drinking when we were in college?"

Brad cringed, hoping his staff would not overhear the detective's recollections. "Yes, I remember. You showed me how to get it by sending my picture and five bucks to some place in Las Vegas."

"Right. Any underage kid in Yakima knows you need fake ID to go out drinking beer. These morons on this side of the mountains just stroll right into this place without identification and order fancy cocktails. And the bigger morons running the place serve them. I simply can't understand some people.

"Oh, I also had her car impounded right after I got back to work following my lunch visit here last week. I wanted to get it checked out. That really pissed her off because she had to ride the light rail to work for three days. I told her she shouldn't be driving a big rig like that to work in city traffic, anyway. Wastes too much gas. It never ceases to amaze me how the people of this city claim to be so green, and yet they drive their cars in one of the worst traffic jams in the country every day. Real hypocrites. Anyway, telling her she was contributing to the problem didn't help her mood any. She said she couldn't care less about how much gas she wastes because she can afford it. Great attitude. She'd never get by in Yakima acting like that."

"What were you looking for on the car?"

"Some reason it could put out enough carbon monoxide in three minutes to knock her out. Like you said, it didn't make sense. With the catalytic converters on cars these days, they hardly put out any carbon monoxide.

You can still poison yourself in a garage, but it takes forever. But when I heard about the guy hanging around the parking lot at Green Lake and her car ran rough after she left there, it made me wonder if he had ripped off her catalytic converter."

"Why would he do that?"

"Well, Doc, one reason would be so her car puts out a lot of carbon monoxide and she kills herself. Slip over to her garage during the night, duct tape the edges of the big garage door, and disconnect the garage door opener. She comes in, fires up the big rig, can't open the garage door, and bingo!"

"You said that was one reason. Is there another reason people take catalytic converters?"

"Boy, for a guy who knows so much, you sure don't know much. Didn't you take auto shop in high school?"

"They didn't offer auto shop at Mercer Island High School."

"Oh yeah, I forgot. Well every guy graduating from high school in Yakima knows all about catalytic converters. They are loaded with small amounts of precious metals like platinum, palladium, and rhodium. You can sell one to a metal recycler for about two hundred bucks. Thieves target vehicles like SUVs and pickup trucks because they are easier to crawl under. With a battery-powered reciprocating saw, a good operator can cut one out of the exhaust system and be gone in about three minutes."

"Was her catalytic converter gone?"

"No, it was there. In fact, her vehicle's carbon monoxide emissions were fine. You were probably right about one thing."

"That's reassuring to know. What was I right about?'

"Her car was probably running rough because the ten-dollar-a-gallon gas had some water in it. Her car is running fine now. Also, hardly any gas had been used from her tank since she filled it the night before. It was not running for hours before she walked into the garage. I still think the condo manager is a suspect, though. I'm having him watched. Now you know everything I found out."

Brad stared at his friend, trying to digest all the information the detective had unearthed. He finally spoke. "It sounds to me like someone tried to murder this woman by poisoning her with carbon monoxide. There must have been an extremely high level in the garage when she walked in because she lost consciousness so quickly and had such a high level in her blood. Someone apparently entered the garage sometime before 7:00 a.m., put tape around the garage door, and filled the space with carbon monoxide from a source other than her car. But who? Why? How?"

"I don't know the answers to those questions. But I agree someone was trying to knock her off. I sent an evidence team over to her garage today to look for anything I might have missed and dust for prints. I'll figure it out. Thanks for calling me. Now, can we go to the hospital cafeteria again?"

Chapter 15

B rad was in the middle of a run on the Burke-Gilman Trail near Sand Point when his cell phone rang. The hospital operator at Metro connected his cell phone call to the county paramedic triage center.

"This is Dr. Franklin, Medical Director of Metropolitan Hyperbaric. Is someone looking for me?"

A critical care fellow from the University of Washington program usually manned the triage phone on Saturday afternoons, moonlighting to supplement his or her meager salary as a physician-in-training.

"Yes, Dr. Franklin, I am calling you about a fifty-five-year-old diver just picked up by medics. He was diving this afternoon at Edmonds Underwater Park. It was his first dive of the day, and apparently, the first dive of his career following scuba certification. He is said to have appeared confused after fifteen minutes at a depth of forty feet. During a controlled ascent assisted by his dive buddy, he lost consciousness, had his mouthpiece fall out, and likely inhaled seawater before he stopped breathing."

"What was he like when they got him to shore?"

"Thready pulse, blood pressure eighty over palp. Bystanders were doing rescue breathing when the medics arrived. After they intubated him and started bagging, he coughed up a bunch of frothy, blood-tinged sputum. Does this sound like pulmonary barotrauma with an arterial gas embolism?"

Brad weighed the possibilities. Arterial gas embolism is always mentioned as a possibility when a diver loses consciousness during ascent. When a diver who has been breathing compressed air underwater ascends toward the surface, the water pressure on him becomes less and the gas in his lungs expands. If the diver holds his breath during that process, the expanding gas can tear his lung tissue, allowing bubbles to enter the bloodstream and obstruct blood flow to critical organs, including the brain.

In this instance, it didn't make sense because the diver became confused initially at depth, not while ascending through the water column. Statistically, previously unrecognized heart disease was the more likely cause for this diver's episode since he was over fifty years old.

As he built a mental list of possibilities comprising the diver's differential diagnosis, Brad mused the diver could have experienced a heart attack as a result of poor blood flow to his heart muscle through narrowed coronary arteries. This could result in pulmonary edema or fluid in the lungs. Secondly, pulmonary edema during diving could be caused by a heart rhythm disturbance. Finally, he could have developed a syndrome recently described in diving medical literature called pulmonary edema of immersion, wherein susceptible individuals have been seen to develop recurrent episodes of fluid in the lungs despite normal heart function.

"I doubt this was a gas embolism because he was not ascending when the symptoms began. It sounds like he developed progressively dropping oxygen levels, probably from cardiac disease. Even though he doesn't appear to have a condition that would benefit from treatment in the hyperbaric chamber, have the transporting paramedics take him straight to the emergency department at Metropolitan anyway. Bypass the county hospital trauma unit, despite what the director there may advise you. An injured diver needs to be in a place with the expertise to care for him, and I need to personally confirm the story before I decide he doesn't need to go in the chamber."

"Got it. He's headed your way. Thanks for the help. We don't get too many really sick divers, and it can be a little uncomfortable triaging them over the phone."

"No problem. Call us whenever you have any questions. That's what we are here for. And if you guys want some refresher lectures on diving accidents, give the hyperbaric center a call during the week and we'll set some up."

Chapter 16

Due to traffic congestion on 25th Avenue NE resulting from the early-September non-conference college football game underway in Husky Stadium, it took Brad thirty minutes to get to the hospital. By the time he arrived, the patient was already in ED Room 2. En route to the hospital, he had called the day's hyperbaric charge nurse, Earl Washington.

Earl's role in the Hyperbaric Department was the same as Patti's. Each worked six days in a row, then took eight days off, in a complimentary schedule. They coordinated and oversaw all the treatments, routine and emergent. Since they always worked during the day and took calls at night for emergency treatments, Earl and Patti were at risk for sleep deprivation. Brad was aware of this and silently assessed their alertness any time there had been an emergency the preceding night.

Earl lived on First Hill close to Metropolitan and was

already at the patient's bedside when Brad walked in. Earl appeared rested and alert.

"Hi Earl. Thanks for coming in so quickly. If the story I heard is correct, he won't need recompression. But I wanted to get the facts myself. You know the story is always different third-hand."

"No worries. I got here about ten minutes ago and had a chance to scope things out. I've even talked to his dive buddy, who is in the waiting room."

The patient lying on the stretcher between them was a middle-aged male, unconscious from sedating medication, intubated and being mechanically ventilated. He still wore his obviously new wetsuit, raggedly cut apart by the medics down to his waist. On his left forearm was a tattoo of the mushroom cloud of a nuclear explosion.

"This is Floyd Ashton," began Earl. "He is fifty-five years old, in apparently good health, and just completed Open Water scuba certification last month. He is co-owner of one of those salmon farms and took diving lessons because he wanted to show off the operation to others from below. His dive buddy gave me his certification card. His instructor's name is on the back. Claude taught him to dive."

He showed the wallet-sized plastic C-Card documenting basic scuba certification to Brad.

"According to the ER doc here, his chest x-ray shows aspiration of seawater versus pulmonary edema or a combination of both. Breathing 100% oxygen on the ventilator, his arterial blood gases show an oxygen partial pressure of 55 mm Hg. That doesn't seem too good, but his pulse oximeter saturation is 97%, so everyone is okay with it."

"Thanks for the excellent summary, Earl. Let's see if we can figure out what happened to Floyd out there at Edmonds Underwater Park this morning."

Chapter 17

After they had finished examining Floyd and reviewed his digital chest x-ray on the ER monitor, Brad said, "Let's go talk to Mr. Ashton's dive buddy. I need to ask him a couple of questions."

"Correction. His dive buddy is a her, not a him. And wait until you meet her."

Earl escorted a young woman into the conference room off the ED waiting room. "Candy, meet Dr. Bradley Franklin. Dr. Franklin, this is Ms. Candice Mays. She was Mr. Ashton's dive buddy today."

While Brad shook hands with her, he thought Candy could be no more than twenty-five years old. She was close to six feet tall and wore a hot pink thong bikini with a white fishnet shirt over it. Her short hair was bleached almost white, she had obvious breast augmentation, and she spoke with a strong Southern drawl, likely Atlanta. Her entire body had the type of deep tan you can only achieve by religious attendance at a tanning parlor, possibly employing a personal tanning trainer.

"Pleased to meet you, Dr. Franklin. You may call me Candy. All my regulars do. How can I help?"

"If you don't mind my asking, Candy, how did you come to be Floyd's dive buddy?"

"I've known Floyd for about two months. I'm a professional dancer, and he comes into the bar where I work every Friday and Saturday night. He's very wealthy, you know. He owns a chain of shrimp farms in China and has a fleet of shrimp boats in the Gulf of Mexico. He lives on Mercer Island. Anyway, he convinced me to take diving lessons with him so we could go look at his salmon farm underwater. We just graduated. This was our first dive without an instructor."

"I see," said Brad, not intending the pun. He found it difficult to keep his eyes at the level of the horizon. "Can you tell me what happened today?"

"Well, Floyd suggested I spend the night at his place last night so we could get an early start this morning. We went to his place right after I got off at 2:00 a.m. This morning, when we were loading all of our gear into his rig, Floyd realized he had dropped off our scuba tanks to be filled but had forgotten to pick them up. So we made a brief detour to get them. There are no dive shops on Mercer Island, you know. They aren't upscale enough for the community.

"Did you know there are five Starbucks stores within four blocks of his apartment building? Anyway, after we picked up the tanks, we drove to Edmonds, got suited up, and waded in at the underwater park near the ferry terminal. We were following the sea bottom out, and Floyd kept goofing around. Pinching me on the behind and the like. He is such a flirt. At forty feet, he suddenly stopped putting his hands all over me, and I turned to look at him. His eyes were sort of glazed over, and he wasn't responding to me. We started up, and he breathed in some water. Once we got to the surface, some other divers came to help him, and I didn't see what happened until he left in the ambulance."

"Why didn't you see?"

"Well it turns out one of the other divers at the Edmonds Underwater Park today is also a regular customer where I work. I was so surprised and happy to see Garry, I forgot all about Floyd. Garry is such a nice guy. He is a former firefighter, so he was willing to help me peel off my tight wetsuit. He even found my net top for me and drove me to the hospital. Unfortunately, Garry doesn't live on Mercer Island."

"Wow," exclaimed Brad under his breath. "Earl, that's all the information I need. Tell the ED doc Mr. Ashton doesn't need hyperbaric treatment, and he should be managed in the critical care unit as a potential cardiac case with saltwater aspiration. Candy, you've been most helpful."

"Oh, Dr. Franklin, the pleasure has been all mine. Remember, if you come in before 8:00 p.m. and buy two drinks, there is no cover charge."

Brad smiled at her and turned to address the hyperbaric nurse. "Earl, the ED always draws several extra tubes of blood. Please contact the lab and if any are leftover for Mr. Ashton, ask them to hold one blood sample tube with a red top and two tubes with green tops. That way, we'll have more than one sample type in case we think of something we want to measure later. I'll call Dr. Tom Steves on the East Coast Monday morning and see if Mr. Ashton would be a good subject for his new study on the mechanisms of decompression sickness. Since Floyd was diving but does not appear to have decompression sickness, I think he may fit into the control group if I remember the study's entry criteria correctly. I'll also find out what type of blood samples Dr. Steves needs for the study. We can get consent from Floyd to send his blood if and when he recovers."

The two men again thanked Candy for her assistance as she prepared to leave. Earl wistfully watched her walk down the hall. "Boy, this is one time I wish I owned a car. I'll bet she needs a ride home."

Brad smiled. "Earl, you are so considerate."

Chapter 18

Before coming to the Metro Hyperbaric Department, Earl had worked as a critical care nurse at Northgate Hospital in Seattle, the same hospital in which he had been born thirty-eight years earlier. He loved everything about the Pacific Northwest and was teased mercilessly by his co-workers because he had never been outside the states of Washington, Idaho, and Oregon. His attitude was, "If you live in God's country, why leave it?"

Earl was obsessively green, sorting his trash into yard waste recycling (which included pizza boxes) and conventional recycling. He never bought water in plastic bottles, organized beach cleanups around Puget Sound, and gave lectures to Scout troops about environmental projects they could undertake. He rode a bike and when he had to travel any distance, only went by public transportation.

As he entered the quiet Hyperbaric Department early on Monday morning, Earl was still the charge nurse. He saw Claude working on one of the chamber lights.

"Claude, I see you are still teaching scuba diving," he said, fumbling with both hands in the deep pockets of his white lab coat, searching for something.

"Of course I am. Best instructor in town. I just wish I had more time for it but working here is what pays the rent. Why do you mention it?"

"I've got something here that you will be interested to see."

"Hey, is that someone's C-card?"

"Yeah, on Saturday Brad and I saw the card's owner in the ED being evaluated for a diving accident. His dive buddy gave it to me. You trained Mr. Floyd Ashton, didn't you?"

"Oh, my God, I sure did. Impossible to forget him. You don't actually train old Floyd because he believes he already knows it all. He's one of those polluting salmon farmers out in the Sound. Bragged a lot about how great that big BP oil spill was because he made a bunch of money doing nothing."

"And Candy Mays was in the class, too?"

"You better believe it. Also impossible to forget. A bimbo strip club dancer who Floyd kept interested in him by making up stories about his Chinese shrimp farms and Gulf Coast fishing fleets. On a personal level, Floyd is a likeable enough guy. I went to the Roanoke on Mercer Island with him for a few beers and heard the whole story of how he ended up in Seattle. It's pretty wild. Do you have any time?"

"Yeah, I have about ten minutes until I need to start checking in the patients. None of them are here yet. Go ahead."

"Well, Floyd is a real operator. Before moving to Seattle, he made some quick money down in the Gulf after the giant oil spill resulted from a leaking British Petroleum well. At the time the spill began, he was using his thirty-two-year-old fishing boat, *High Hopes Herbie*, to take cash-paying tourists out for a day of deep sea fishing off the coast of Louisiana.

"In the days immediately after the spill started, there was chaos as BP fought to seal the leak and contain the spill that began to drift across the Gulf of Mexico. The company had an immediate need for skippered boats willing to work round the clock seven days a week to move small equipment, ferry workers from shore to ships or platforms, and be available for immediate dispatch on whatever task was needed. Floyd gambled long and won big. He signed a contract to provide all those services at $250 per hour 24/7 until the spill was capped, payable whether his boat and crew were being used or simply available on call. Since he had no crew outside of a single Mexican deckhand named Juan, whose job was to help the tourists with their fishing lines, there was no way he would be able to fulfill the contract requirements for more than a few days before needing sleep.

"As it turned out, overeager and scared BP representatives contracted many more boats than were needed. After a few hectic days in the immediate aftermath of the initial well explosion, *High Hopes Herbie* ended up anchored most of the time. Floyd dozed on the deck in the sunshine much of the day, while Juan maintained the boat. Floyd occasionally ferried some workers or scientists about but *Herbie* generally went unused and Floyd undisturbed. When the leaking well was finally capped three months later, Floyd cashed in his hours for almost half a million dollars. He sold his old boat and paid Juan only $5,000, which represented three-months pay at $1,000 per month, plus a $2,000 bonus for working 90 days without a day off. Then he fired Juan and moved to Seattle."

Earl stared at Claude in disbelief. "Wow, this guy is really a scammer. Doesn't he have any remorse taking advantage of an ecological disaster like that? Amazing. But I thought he was a fish farmer, not a fishing boat operator."

"His little maneuver during the oil spill may impress you, but you haven't heard the 'Best of Floyd' yet. One of the tourists who fished on his boat in the Gulf prior to the spill told him about salmon farming in Puget Sound. Floyd was intrigued and came up here to investigate. After arriving in Seattle, Floyd rented an apartment at the north end of Mercer Island. Even though living on Mercer Island gave him great access into Seattle on the six lanes of the Interstate-90 floating bridge, neither the beautiful scenery on the island nor the easy downtown access attracted Floyd. He thought living in an affluent suburb on an island in the middle of Lake Washington would be good for his image."

"But Mercer Island is so expensive. How could he afford to live there? I guess because he had half a million bucks," thought Earl out loud, answering his own question.

"Oh, Floyd never paid the going rate if he could avoid it. And the price turned out to be cheap, believe it or not. Despite having the highest property values of any neighborhood in the city, apartments were a bargain on Mercer Island when Floyd arrived in town several months ago. Three independent groups of outside investors had coincidentally and unknowingly each constructed a large building of high-end luxury apartments within blocks of each other. All three complexes opened within the few weeks before Floyd's arrival in town. As a result of a relative glut of executive one-bedroom apartments renting for $3,500 per month, occupancy rates were low.

"Floyd said he was staying in some two-star airport hotel and read about the Mercer Island apartment glut in the business section of the *Seattle Times* newspaper while eating breakfast in a greasy diner next door. He said by the end of the day, he had visited the rental office of all three complexes, bargained with them against each other, and ended up getting the first three months rent-free in exchange for signing a one-year lease, plus a complimentary weeklong vacation in Honolulu's Waikiki Beach."

Earl said, "I want to hear the rest of the 'Best of Floyd' story, but I need to get set up for the first morning treatment. Let's have lunch together and you can finish filling me in."

"You got it."

Chapter 19

E arl met Claude outside the hospital entrance as they had scheduled.

"How did the morning treatments go, Earl?"

"Oh, nothing remarkable. Did another twelve pack. All I could think about was hearing the rest of your 'Best of Floyd,'" smiled Earl. "The stuff you told me this morning was unbelievable."

The two co-workers walked down Madison Street to the tiny Polish delicatessen they both loved. The deli's proprietor smoked his own meats and sausages on site, even though the shop was located in downtown Seattle. Each purchased a made-to-order sandwich at the counter, then they picked up cans of soda and walked two blocks to Freeway Park, the city park built over I-5. It was a beautiful late summer day, with clear skies and a comfortable temperature of seventy-two degrees. If the weather and the department's emergency treatment schedule allowed, the hyperbaric staff liked to get outdoors and enjoy the sun whenever possible. The days were already growing shorter, and they knew with Seattle's northern latitude, the time was coming when daylight would be a valued commodity.

After settling themselves on an open concrete bench in the park, they began to eat sandwiches of soft sourdough bread heaped with Krakow sausage, lettuce, tomatoes, and pickles. Claude continued his story.

"Floyd googled 'fish farming' and found an organization named something like the Washington Fish Growers Association. Their site provided links to salmon farming operations in Puget Sound. He visited several farms in the area."

"What exactly is a salmon farm? I've heard of them but have never seen one. I know lots of people who don't think the salmon from one tastes as good as the wild ones."

"Oh, when I was in the navy at Keyport, I saw plenty of salmon farms in the Sound. A giant floating pen is constructed out of netting and anchored to the seafloor. About 50,000 fish are raised in it together. They are fed with fish pellets from above. And you're right. Many Seattleites eating dinner in a restaurant will ask where their salmon came from and order something else if it is farm-raised.

"There is also widespread discussion about the environmental impact of using these pens, which are also known as aquaculture. The incredible density of fish per unit of water volume produces significant amounts of waste, discharged directly into the water. This includes the antibiotics and pesticides they need to feed to the fish to suppress infections resulting from the crowded quarters. It does not help that Puget Sound flushes more like a bathtub than a toilet. Even worse, when some of the farmed fish inevitably escape the pens, they compete with wild salmon for food. If they mate with wild fish, the genetic diversity of the population could be reduced."

"Sounds like a very non-green enterprise."

"You've got that right. But Floyd outdid even himself. He invested in a company that was going to try raising genetically modified salmon that would grow at three times their normal rate."

"And produce three times as much waste, dump three times as much antibiotics in the water, and cause three times as many problems when they escape?" Earl shook his head.

"Now you're understanding. Floyd doesn't care about being green. He made a chunk of money on a man-made environmental disaster. The only green on Floyd's radar screen is the kind he can fold and put into his wallet."

Earl was disgusted. "Now that I know more, it is obvious this guy is an environmental disaster."

"You're right," agreed Claude. "But to Floyd it was just business and the pursuit of a quick buck. Many people would be offended by his lack of ecological concern—hey, what happened to Floyd anyway? You said you saw him in the ER Saturday with Brad and got his C-card from Candy. Did he get bent already?"

"We're not sure what occurred, but he didn't have the bends. Something happened to him only a few minutes after he and Candy got to forty feet out at Edmonds. He became confused at depth, then lost consciousness on the way up and aspirated. Brad thinks it was a cardiac event. We didn't treat him because his dive profile did not give him a significant enough nitrogen load for the bends and because his central nervous system symptoms started before beginning ascent."

"Did he die?"

"No, but he is in the CCU on a ventilator with a focal myocardial infarction and diffuse heart muscle dysfunction. I went by and saw him today. The CCU is one hectic place. The cardiology team cathed him and found clean coronaries. Pretty interesting. He must have had coronary spasms. They say he'll probably do okay."

"That's too bad," muttered Claude. He suddenly realized how he must have sounded. "I mean it's too bad he is sick and all."

"Oh, I know exactly what you mean. Now I realize how those salmon farmers are polluting the Sound and leaving the rest of us to deal with it while they reap the profits. It reminds me of when I was a kid and rode the ferries across Puget Sound with my folks. The highlight of the trip was watching the crew empty the trash bins off the back while the ferry was underway."

"Wow," responded Claude. "I never realized you were so passionate about the environment."

"Someone has to be!"

"That's true," said Claude.

The two walked over to the garbage can where they tossed their sandwich wrappers and then started walking back up the hill to Metro. They carried their aluminum soda cans for recycling.

Chapter 20

A few hours later, Brad chatted with the staff in the chamber area after wrapping up the last routine hyperbaric treatment of the day. Bob strolled in.

"Am I interrupting anything important, Doc?"

"No, we were just shooting the breeze before closing up shop. Did you learn anything more about Laurie Rodgers?"

"Yes, in fact I did. But I'd like to talk in your office."

The two men walked down the hall to Brad's office.

Once they had closed the door and settled into chairs, Bob said, "I need to keep my cards close to my vest since this has become an official investigation."

"Sure, I understand."

Bob asked, "Do you know how she is doing these days? I called her and she said she was fine, but I want to make sure you agree."

"She is back to normal. I saw her in clinic for follow-up

six weeks after her poisoning event, and she looked fine. I sent her for a neuropsychological testing battery because of the short-term memory loss she experienced at the time of the poisoning. She did well in every category. As we would say in the business, she appears to have sustained no permanent neurological sequelae from the poisoning—exactly the goal of hyperbaric oxygen treatment for this condition."

"Good. I'm glad to hear it. My investigation points to the attempted murderer probably being a Boeing employee."

"Wow! Now how in the world did you come to that conclusion?"

"Well, I told you I was having an evidence team go through her garage with a fine-tooth comb. They were very excited about the duct tape. As you know, duct tape is sticky stuff and very tough. When I was growing up in Yakima, we used it to repair everything. It was especially useful in patching up holes rusted through your muffler."

"I suppose you learned that in auto shop."

"Nah. Common knowledge. Anyway, this roll was no usual duct tape. It was 400-miles-per-hour duct tape."

"400 miles per hour?"

"It turns out Boeing has metal duct tape they sometimes use to patch up planes. Depending on the application, they need duct tape of different strengths and stickiness. This happened to be aerospace industry duct tape rated for 400 miles per hour, not the stuff you or I could buy at Home Depot. Or would want to buy. Costs about two hundred dollars a roll."

"So I understand the Boeing connection, but how many people work there?"

"Unfortunately for my investigation, but fortunate for the Seattle economy, there are tens of thousands. But there was another clue I thought you might be able to help me with. What do you know about charcoal briquettes and carbon monoxide?"

"Quite a bit. We frequently treat patients with carbon monoxide poisoning associated with the indoor use of charcoal. Most of the time it occurs in association with a storm that knocks out power, and people bring charcoal into the house as an alternate source of heat or for cooking. All burning produces carbon monoxide, but a smoldering burn produces the most. And charcoal does just that—smolder. It is occasionally used in this country to attempt suicide, but the practice is much more common in the Far East. It is the second most common method of suicide in Hong Kong and widely publicized there."

"That's very helpful. Remember we concluded there must have been a lot of carbon monoxide in her garage when she entered, and it could not have come from her car?"

"Sure. In light of her blood level and loss of consciousness in minutes, the level must have been at least 1,000 parts per million in the garage when she walked in."

"My team discovered a one-gallon tin can in the corner of the garage with about two inches of ash in the bottom of it. They took it back to the lab and determined the ash was from charcoal. The technicians then burned some charcoal out in the parking lot and weighed the ash. They estimate someone burned about two pounds in the can. When I called Ms. Rodgers recently, she claimed to know nothing about it. Says she doesn't even have a charcoal grill. My questions for you are these. Is that enough charcoal to produce a large amount of carbon monoxide? And second, wouldn't she have noticed the smoke in the garage when she walked in? When I barbeque burgers, black smoke pours out of my grill."

"To answer your first question, two pounds of charcoal is plenty to raise the carbon monoxide level in the garage that high, even with loss through the walls and doors. I read one estimate that one and one-half pounds burned indoors will raise the carbon monoxide level of an average one-bedroom apartment to the 10,000 parts per million range. A pound of charcoal could even have been burned in the garage hours before she entered since the bigger leaks were sealed with tape.

"To answer your second question, burning charcoal alone produces very little smoke. Think about it. You light your charcoal, and then wait until the briquettes have turned gray all over before putting on your steak. Or hamburger, as the case may be. At that moment, there is almost no visible smoke and carbon monoxide is odorless and colorless. After you put your meat on the grill, the burning grease dripping onto the coals produces the smoke. So, yes, Detective, she could have walked into a garage filled with carbon monoxide from burning charcoal and not noticed it until she passed out."

"Okay. Great! No time for the cafeteria today. I'm off to find someone who works at Boeing and has roots or ties to Hong Kong."

"Good luck, Bud. You might look up our old college friend, Jerry Chinn. I think he still works at Boeing down in Renton. He might be able to offer you some guidance."

"Jerry Chinn? Now, there's a thought. Really smart guy."

Chapter 21

"Brad, Taylor Marks is waiting in your office," Cathy said as Brad walked into the department and past her desk.

"Thanks for the heads-up." Brad knew something more than the usual finance discussion was on the agenda since Marks usually attended the weekly meeting for upper-level administrators from 7:00 to 8:00 on Tuesday mornings.

He opened the door to his office. His administrative partner sat in one of the side chairs and looked very serious.

"Good morning, Taylor. If you are here about yesterday afternoon's new monthly budget numbers, I've been a little busy lately and have not had time to look at them."

"I'm here on other business, Brad. The budget numbers for last month look great. Will you shut the door?"

Brad closed the door, took off his jacket, and hung it on the hook behind. He settled into his desk chair.

"Then, what can I do for you?"

"The CEO asked me to find out if you are in some kind of trouble."

"Why in the world would he think that?"

"This is not common knowledge, but the hospital started installing security cameras and facial recognition software this month to insure inpatients who are confused do not inadvertently wander off their floors or even outdoors. They began installation on the ground floor because a confused patient wandering out of the hospital would be bad news. They are working up floor by floor."

"And you are here because the system saw me leaving the hospital too early last night?"

"Brad, this is serious. The system recognized an undercover Seattle policeman in the cafeteria with you two times in the past week. Security reported it to the CEO, and I was asked to sort it out. Are you being investigated for something?"

"It's not what you think. Boy, there really are no secrets in a hospital, are there? I called the detective in myself to investigate some suspicious circumstances surrounding one of our patients. We had lunch together because he is my old college roommate."

"Why didn't you notify risk management instead?"

"Because I needed a policeman, not a lawyer."

"Tell me about the case."

"Taylor, I can't. It would be a HIPPA violation."

"At least tell me the issue is resolved."

"I can't do that, either. It may be just beginning."

"Well, then at least warn me the next time you are going to call the police into Metro. I don't like being summoned to the CEO's office and have no idea what he wants to talk about."

"Okay, I'll do that. And I'll get to the budget numbers sometime this week. I'll drop you an e-mail if I see anything out of whack."

"I've got your back, Brad."

"I'm sure you do, Taylor. I'm sure you do."

Chapter 22

B rad walked to the chamber area and sat at the nursing station next to Earl.

"Guess who I saw in clinic yesterday for his dive accident follow-up appointment?"

"I have no idea. It seems like we treated a couple dozen in the past few months. Was it one I was involved with?"

"Yep. Floyd Ashton."

"So, Floyd made it? That's great, I guess. Was Candy with him?"

"No, it was just Floyd. He's doing well. He was in the hospital for about two weeks. After they diuresed him, the CCU team was able to extubate him and get him off the ventilator relatively easily. He did have an unusual complication a couple of days after he was admitted to the unit. One morning the left side of his body went weak, like he had a stroke. The cap on his central line was missing, and the catheter into his jugular vein was sucking in air. They took him for a brain CT scan but did not see any air bubbles in the brain blood vessels. By the time he got back to the unit, his symptoms had resolved. It was attributed to a transient small stroke or TIA. The nurse taking care of him swears the cap was on the line when she went to care for her other patient and was out of the room for thirty minutes. But you have to wonder if a small air embolism caused his symptoms."

"No one was seen fooling with his lines, were they?"

"No, they had just called a code on another patient in the unit and all attention was directed there. Anyway, he recovered, went out to the cardiac floor, then to in-patient rehabilitation. After discharge, he was referred to Metro's outpatient cardiac rehab program and apparently participated religiously. A repeat echocardiogram was done last week, and it showed he has recovered his cardiac function."

"It's good to know they did not discover a hospital staff member intentionally trying to harm him by uncapping his central line."

"To intentionally allow air into someone's central line to cause an air embolism would first require the person work at the hospital to gain unrestricted access to the CCU, and second, have critical care experience so they knew what they were doing. I think that's unlikely in this case. It's amazingly coincidental, but the hospital was in the process of installing security cameras with facial recognition software on each unit. Even though it was still in test mode when Floyd's episode occurred, they were able to review the file from the CCU during the day of Floyd's event at my request."

"What did they find?" Earl asked, as he stared at Brad.

"I was told the program identified only hospital employees and a handful of patient family members entering or leaving the unit, none of whom were relations of Floyd. And Candy didn't visit."

"This was probably a random event. Floyd dodged a couple bullets with this one didn't he?" Earl asked.

"Yep, he sure did. I told him if he were a cat, he would have used up two of his nine lives. I returned his C-card to him."

"You didn't clear him to return to diving, did you?

"Of course not. I told him when a person almost dies on their first dive, someone is trying to tell them something. Especially when we really don't understand exactly what happened. I said from a diving medicine standpoint, he should never dive again. But you know, I'm not the diving police and have no power to prevent him from diving. Once a diver is certified, he is approved for life. His C-card never expires."

"Do you think he will follow your advice?"

"No doubt about it. Old Floyd had no fun during this experience. He said he has sworn off diving for life."

"You asked me to remind you to see if he would consent to have his blood samples sent to Dr. Steves for his diver microparticle study if he survived."

"Oh, that's right. I did talk to Tom Steves on the phone when Floyd was in the hospital. He said Floyd would be an ideal control subject and asked me to send one red and one green top blood tube. I forgot to ask Floyd about it yesterday. Thanks for reminding me. I'll call Floyd this afternoon to get his consent. I still can't get over that mushroom cloud tattoo on his arm. In the meantime, will you call the lab and see if they still have his frozen blood samples? I'll let you know when I have gotten his approval and you can have them sent out."

"Okay, Doc. And thanks for the follow-up. I always like to know what happens to our patients."

Chapter 23

As Brad walked to work at Metro, he thought about how Seattle's annual "drought" was about to end. It was almost Halloween, the date by which the region's "Indian summer" had usually ended. The misty winter rains would soon begin and continue to fall on what sometimes seemed to be the majority of days until May.

In some parts of the United States, men consider it to be effeminate to carry and use an umbrella, an act beneath their masculine personas. In Seattle, umbrella use is not considered effeminate—it is considered practical.

He entered the department and glanced toward the chamber area. It was apparent there had been emergency treatments during the night. He noticed that there were too many staff present for this hour in the morning, and some of them were busy sanitizing chamber stretchers or packing used linens into overflowing wheeled hampers for soiled laundry.

Dr. Guy Stolp was typing a patient note at one of the nursing station computers. Guy was another hyperbaric physician supervised by Brad. He sat down silently next to Guy, waiting for him to finish. He knew how hard it was to write or dictate a succinct patient note with interruptions.

Brad had known Guy a long time, since his fellowship training years at Duke University. It never ceased to amaze him when he recalled Guy's academic history. After growing up surfing the waves rolling onto the beaches of Southern California, he had majored in beach volleyball at the University of Santa Barbara. At least that's how Guy told the story. Brad doubted Guy rarely studied because his next accomplishment was receipt of a Fulbright Scholarship leading to a master's degree in human biology at Oxford. Guy was a new junior faculty member at Duke when Brad arrived there for training. They became acquainted through a collaborative research project. Even though Guy was a few years older than Brad and a couple of steps further down the career path, they became good friends at "Mr. Duke's Place," as some of the elderly patients referred to the academic institution built by the tobacco magnate.

When Brad finished training and was recruited to Metropolitan Hospital in Seattle, Guy followed in about a year. Brad suspected it was to escape the politics of academia, but Guy claimed he moved because he didn't like to "stay in one place too long." In spite of that, he had been at Metro for over a decade, practicing anesthesia part-time and hyperbaric medicine part-time. When he practiced hyperbaric medicine, Brad was now his boss—at least on the organizational chart.

Guy finished on the computer and turned to his colleague. "Good morning. Busy hyperbaric night on call. We just finished treating a family of four for carbon monoxide poisoning. Lots of media coverage. Did you hear about it on the news while you were driving in?"

"No, because I walk in. And today was fresh croissant day. I bought a few extra. You can find them in the staff lounge."

"Oh yeah, I forgot. I knew there was some reason I was glad you walked to work. Anyway, this family was poisoned in a house fire. They got out before fire spread to the bedroom area of the home, thanks to a carbon monoxide alarm."

"Chalk up another one for the legislation mandating them in all residences in Washington State." Brad knew all about the legislation because he had helped lobby the state legislature on the issue two years earlier. "A house fire is interesting, but it's not really very newsworthy. Why were so many media here?"

"This was no ordinary house fire. Remember the controversy last year when the Nature Conservancy was raising money to buy the plot of land along Lake Union for a wildlife preserve? The rich guy from Vancouver, British Columbia, heard about it and bought it out from under them?"

"Yes, the guy who made so much money growing medical cannabis for all of Canada. He bought the last piece of undeveloped land along the lake while they ran their fundraising campaign. Really irritating."

"Well, even more irritating to some people has been the fact he is building a 20,000 square foot, $100 million house on it. For four people!"

"I heard about the mega-house on the news a few weeks ago. Wasn't some eco-terrorist group threatening to burn it down if construction continued?"

"Yeah, the Earth Protection Organization. Since they preach nonviolence, they probably thought the house was not occupied yet as it is still under construction."

"Is the family okay?"

"I think so. Three of them had loss of consciousness with the carbon monoxide exposure but all four were asymptomatic by the end of the treatment. I'm having those three come back for a second treatment this afternoon. Then they can probably go home."

"How is the house?"

"Oh, the family will have to go back home to Canada. The house is a total loss. It will take a couple of years to rebuild, if they decide to do it."

"Or, the guy could donate the land to the Nature Conservancy and stay out of Seattle." Earl had been listening to the physicians' conversation while straightening up the nursing station for the coming day.

That's unlikely to happen, Brad thought silently, a little surprised at how vocal Earl was on the topic.

Chapter 24

Randy and Claude climbed onto empty bar stools at a popular student watering hole on 45th Avenue Northeast, about a mile from the campus. The University of Washington had been back in autumn session for three weeks, and as the two knew, it also meant students, including co-eds, had returned from summer break to populate the University District in Seattle. The bar was dark, filled with pool tables, each illuminated by a single bare light bulb hanging from a wire from the ceiling. "China Grove" by the Doobie Brothers blared from giant loud speakers suspended in each corner of the room. Every pool table was occupied, and rows of quarters along the edge of each showed the number of games reserved in advance. Couples sat in booths around the edge of the room, pouring beer into their glasses from pitchers, eating greasy cheeseburgers with even greasier fries, and talking.

A bouncer sat at the entry door, manned even though it was a quiet Saturday afternoon. His short hair and clean-cut, chiseled facial features made him look like a marine home on leave. He wore a polo shirt bearing the logo of the establishment. His tanned biceps stretched the short sleeves tight and the massive muscles of his upper chest did likewise with the body of the shirt. Watching him work, Randy remarked he must be at least six-feet five-inches tall, since he looked prospective patrons in the eye even while sitting on a stool. The legal age for entry was twenty-one years, and this was one bouncer who apparently intended to make sure the law was obeyed. He carded everyone. The establishment did too much business to take the risk of a license suspension for serving alcohol to minors.

Two co-eds appeared in the doorway, catching the attention of both men instantly. One tall, one short. One blonde, one brunette. Both wore short skirts and tops reading "Pink U," products of Victoria's Secret. Both were pretty. When asked by the bouncer for identification, the young women acted surprised he thought they looked so young and dug around in their handbags, eventually producing what looked like drivers' licenses from twenty feet away.

The guardian of the door pulled out a small flashlight like the ones used at airport security stations by TSA agents. After inspecting each ID card, he smiled at the two young women and they smiled back, extending their hands to accept their cards. The bouncer then shook his head, stacked the two laminated cards on top of each other and tore them in half, a feat neither Randy nor Claude ever would have imagined possible.

The bouncer then tossed the fake ID cards into a large clear glass fishbowl on the table next to him. They had not noticed it on the way in but it must have contained hundreds of pieces of identification, all torn in half. It was clear no one under the age of twenty-one was getting in the door. The two young men sighed with disappointment as the twenty-year-old women turned and walked out into the night.

Those thoughts were short-lived, though, as a ruckus broke out between the men playing pool on the table closest to their stools. Two men about thirty years old shouted at each other, their faces six inches apart. Both wore dirty jeans and t-shirts. One's shirt read "Spotted Owls Taste Like Fried Chicken" on the back. The other's shirt was tie-dyed, like those worn by Bill Walton and other Grateful Dead fans. Everyone in the bar stopped to listen when the yelling started.

"You are an idiot if you don't think this will work!" shouted one, pointing his finger in the face of his companion.

"I keep trying to tell you people will be able to tell the difference and the whole thing will go down!" said the other as he swatted the finger aside.

"If you had gone to college, you might know something. I took psychology while I was at the U. People will believe it is what you tell them it is."

"If this doesn't work, we wasted a hell of a lot of money."

In the next instant, the bouncer was at their sides, grabbed each by the back of the neck, and smacked their foreheads together. Randy and Claude watched from only a few feet away and winced simultaneously when the impact occurred. It reminded Claude of the way the military MPs had treated him when he returned to base late and with a bit too much grog on board.

"Boys," said the towering bouncer, "there will be no arguing or shouting in this establishment. Is that clear?"

The two dazed men looked up at his face, then at each other. "Yes, sir!" peeped one, his voice cracking with fear.

"We promise not to cause any more trouble," said the other as if he were pleading for his life and not simply trying to prevent ejection from a bar.

The bouncer smiled, released his grip on their necks, and walked back to his stool. Elton John's "Saturday Night's Alright for Fighting" played in the background.

Both men silently turned back to the pool table and re-racked the balls.

"Hey, are you guys okay?" asked Claude, stepping off his stool and over to their table. "That was some attention getter he used. By the way, my name is Claude and this is Randy."

"Nice to meet you. My name is Gregg," the Owl Eater said. "Yeah, I'm all right. It was actually our own fault. We've been here playing pool for about three hours. We got into an argument a couple of hours ago, and he told us he was going to crack some heads if we disrupted things again. I didn't know he really meant it."

"I'm Jim," offered the Deadhead, and they all shook hands.

"What in the hell were you guys fighting about?"

"It's a private matter," said Jim the Deadhead. "You wouldn't be interested."

Gregg turned to Jim and tried to whisper to him. "Maybe they want to be our first investors. You know we need more cash to do this well."

The music required him to speak loud enough for Claude and Randy to hear him anyway.

Randy signaled to the barmaid to bring four more beers. "What kind of enterprise are we talking about? We might have a little cash to invest."

It was clear Gregg ran the show. "Listen carefully. Have you ever heard of shade-grown coffee?"

"I've heard of it, but I'm not too sure what it is," replied Randy.

"Well, let me explain since you could become an investor. You know how the locals are so proud they are green, right? Well, the big coffee companies in town have picked up on that and done stuff like make cups from recyclable material instead of Styrofoam."

"What does that have to do with shade-grown coffee?" Claude asked.

"Don't interrupt. I'm getting there. Anyway, when coffee plants were first introduced from Europe to Central America, they were fragile and couldn't tolerate direct sunlight. So they were grown in the shade. The simplest place to do this was on the floor of the rain forests. The canopy formed by the big trees provided shade from the sun. In operations larger than a family farm, they even planted shade trees."

"So?"

"Jeez, you are impatient, aren't you? After a while, they developed some sun-tolerant coffee bushes, which produce three times more beans than the sun–sensitive ones. So, naturally, they started cutting down the forest to grow more coffee and the tree huggers are all upset about it. And that's our angle. We have the tree huggers out there promoting shade-grown coffee because they don't want to see all the rain forest chopped down. As if Jim and I really care about what happens in Central America!"

The Owl Eater continued and asked the hyperbaric co-workers, "Could either of you tell the difference in flavor between shade-grown and the sun-grown stuff?"

"No, probably not. I'm not sure there is any. Why?"

"Jim and I both worked as coffee roasters for a big company in town. When the green coffee beans are roasted to various temperatures, they acquire the flavor coffee drinkers like. In general, the degrees of roasting are light, medium, medium-dark, and dark. With dark roast, it's really hard to taste the origin of the beans because they are almost burned. We don't think most people can tell the difference and we're going to make a fortune because of it."

"How are you going to do that?" asked Randy, wondering where all this was going.

"We are starting our own coffee company. It's called Seattle Shade and is going to sell only dark-roasted coffee beans. We are going to buy sun-grown coffee beans, roast them ourselves, and sell them as 100% shade-grown from a single estate. Since everyone in this city drinks dark roasts, you can't distinguish the origin. No one will know the difference. If we sell the beans a couple of bucks per pound below the price of other shade-grown, we'll corner the market. Since we're really buying the cheaper sun-grown beans, we'll make a mint in this coffee-crazy city."

Claude and Randy thought about it for a moment, and then Randy expressed what both of them were thinking. "Let me get this straight. You are hoping to increase the sales of environmentally unfriendly sun-grown coffee by telling people it is environmentally friendly shade-grown coffee?"

"The only environment I care about is the one in my bank account. Do you want to invest or not? We've got an old gas-fired drum roaster set up in a warehouse room near Boeing Field. Our first order of beans comes in at the Port of Seattle on a ship tomorrow. We plan to roast and grind a bag of green beans first thing Monday morning. We are going to give away about 500 two-ounce vacuum-sealed bags of ground Seattle Shade coffee at the University District Street Fair next weekend to get people hooked. If we had some more cash, we could order another shipment of beans now and do some advertising."

"No thanks," murmured Claude.

Randy shook his head and tossed a ten-dollar bill on the pool table to cover their beers. They walked out, hoping the two young women had gained access to the bar across the street.

Chapter 25

Brad's cell phone rang on the way to work Wednesday morning. The caller ID read "Robert Heimbigner."

"Hi Bob, what's new? Have you found the person who works at Boeing and has Hong Kong connections?"

"Brad, listen to me. Have you seen the breaking news this morning?"

"No, Bob, it's only 7:15. I make a habit of not watching television every waking moment of my life. Is something going on?"

"Yeah, it sure is. We got a tip chop shop parts were being stored in an old warehouse. Our team raided the place at 5:00 a.m. this morning."

"So, did you find a lot of expensive car parts?"

"No. That's why I am calling. No car parts were in the place. But two dead guys were in the warehouse."

"Why are you calling me?"

"I remember you telling me something about cherry

red skin in carbon monoxide poisoning. Is that right?"

"Yes, but it's only seen in people who have lethal carbon monoxide blood levels."

"These guys were as red as cherries in late June in Yakima. Not like Bings or Rainiers or Black Republicans. Red like sour pie cherries. Does that fit?"

"It sure does. Hemoglobin loaded with carbon monoxide is a bright red color, like pie cherries. Have they had blood levels measured yet?"

"No, it just went down a couple of hours ago. Their bodies are on the way to the county medical examiner as we speak. But there were no obvious signs of trauma, bleeding, or other injury."

"What else was in the place?"

"A couple of empty fifty-pound coffee bean bags, a gas-fired roasting machine, and a grinder. One guy was lying on the floor by the roaster and one by the grinder. No evidence of a struggle or attack. They were cold and stiff. Looked like they had been dead for more than a day. A ventilation hood hanging over the equipment was still running. Ductwork ran up and over to the wall, then dumped outdoors above the entrance door."

"Was there any evidence of a source of carbon monoxide other than the gas roaster?"

"None was apparent. But listen to this. The ventilation vent was sealed outside so no air could exit."

"Sealed? With what?"

"Four-hundred-mile-per-hour duct tape. I have a lot on my plate today because of this discovery but tomorrow

I'm heading to Boeing Renton to talk to Jerry Chinn. I didn't talk to him when you suggested it before because I got distracted by some other cases, and Ms. Rodgers was doing fine. Now it appears someone in this city may really be trying to kill people with carbon monoxide and could actually have succeeded in this instance, if that is indeed how these two coffee roasters died."

"Hopefully Jerry Chinn can provide some insight. Will you have the Medical Examiner call me at Metro when he finishes the autopsies?"

"Will do. It may be a day or two because they have been busy lately."

Chapter 26

Brad remembered Jerry Chinn well. Jerry had gone to work at Boeing immediately after graduation from the University of Washington with his bachelor's degree in mechanical engineering. Brad and Jerry had been relatively good friends during their undergraduate years. Because Brad was pre-med and Jerry was pre-engineering for their first two years at the U, they had almost identical lists of prerequisite classes. It seemed they were in the same class or laboratory section for every course they both took—math, calculus, physics, and chemistry. When a new quarter started, each would walk into a classroom and look for the other, fully expecting them to be there. The pre-med students consistently outdid those headed for engineering, but they remained friends anyway. Jerry had an easygoing attitude. "What do I care? All I have to do is pass."

The pre-meds were known as cutthroats, doing anything they could to get another tenth of a point on their course grades because of the relative competitiveness of medical school admission at the time.

As Brad recalled their relationship after college, he realized how much had changed. They had remained in occasional contact over the years, but while Brad continued to take out educational loans to support another ten years of education, Jerry immediately started earning money at Boeing. During their undergraduate years, Jerry's uncle, Gordon Luk, was infamous for seemingly owning all of the low-rent apartments in the U District. Luk was ruthless in his rental contracts and notorious for failing to repair his units. Because he had a virtual monopoly on rental units around the U, moving was very difficult. Luk would simply tell the student wanting to move nothing was available and force them to extend their lease the month before it ended.

When Brad and Jerry crossed paths every few years after college, it seemed to Brad Chinn was following in his uncle's footsteps. He was frugal with his paychecks from Boeing and bought a small apartment building in the Renton area every time he accumulated enough for another down payment. Once he began to have a significant market share of the low-cost rentals in Renton, Jerry raised the rents high enough that the cash flow from his apartment buildings not only covered their costs but also yielded surplus income to allow him to keep buying more real estate. As long as Boeing did not crash again, Brad thought Jerry was set. Because the commuter traffic was so bad in Seattle and so many people worked at the

Renton Boeing facility south of Seattle, he had a captive audience for his rental units. Just like Gordon Luk had when they were in college.

While Jerry was a ruthless businessman, Brad had to admire him. Brad finished his medical training at age thirty-two and began to pay off educational loans with his new income. When Jerry turned thirty-two, he was one-half of the way to his retirement pension at Boeing and already becoming known as the "Gordon Luk of Renton." Brad knew he would have to work as a physician until age ninety to catch up with Jerry. Debt vs. income for ten years had put them in very different financial situations.

Chapter 27

Brad sat with his wife, Kimberly, in the den of their home on Queene Anne Hill while their daughters, Ann and Lynn, were upstairs, ostensibly doing their homework. Brad analyzed research data on his laptop while Kim worked on a quilt she was making for her mother. Kim, originally from Spokane, now worked as a software engineer for Microsoft. They had met as juniors in college when they were physics lab partners. In her senior year, Kim was the UW Homecoming Queen in the autumn and then graduated summa cum laude in the spring. They married after Brad's first year of medical school and all of his still-single friends were envious because of her beauty and intelligence.

"Kim, I was thinking about one of our old college friends today. Do you remember Jerry Chinn?"

She looked up from her project, sighing at the interruption.

"Sure, I shared a few engineering classes with him. Where is he these days? Is he still making rockets at Mr. Boeing's Place, as you and Guy might call it?'"

When William E. Boeing had started The Boeing Company on the shores of Lake Union in 1910, the company made small airplanes out of spruce wood. Boeing subsequently evolved into a multinational corporation in the business of designing, manufacturing, and selling airplanes, rockets and satellites. Boeing was among the largest aircraft manufacturers in the world and the largest exporter in the United States based on dollar value. In 2013, it was the second largest defense contractor in the world.

"Yeah, he still works at Boeing but I don't know what he does there. He has never been able to tell me because it is all classified. Did I ever tell you how I contributed to his classified clearance?"

"Maybe. Remind me."

Kim set her quilting project aside, knowing from experience that she was not going to be able to concentrate on it until Brad finished telling his story.

"I have actual documentation of the event, so I can do better than that. At the time of my residency, all long distance phone calls into or out of the Minneapolis Veteran's Administration Hospital were recorded and transcribed. The administration claimed it was to provide documentation for patient records, but most of us thought it was to keep us from using the federal phone system for free, personal long-distance calls. I saved one of the transcripts all of these years because it was such an unusual call. If I can find it, you can read it."

Brad disappeared down the hall into the den, and Kim heard him digging through his filing cabinet. He returned victorious, clutching a single sheet of yellowed paper in his hand. She could tell from his excited smile he wanted her full attention.

"Here it is. Let me set the stage for you. I was working in the CCU of the Minneapolis Veteran's Administration Hospital during my residency when I received an urgent overhead page to call the operator.

"The operator said, 'Dr. Franklin, I have a caller on the line who says he is with the FBI and is asking for you.'"

Brad handed Kim an ancient carbon copy paper, with the lines single-spaced in blue ink.

Kim read the transcript aloud.

This is Dr. Brad Franklin.

Hello. My name is Marv Gardens and I work with the FBI Federal Security Clearance Unit. Is this the Bradley Franklin who grew up on Mercer Island, then attended the University of Washington for undergraduate and medical school?

Yes. Am I in some sort of trouble?

No, but you will be if you don't let me ask the questions. Now, did you know an engineering student named Jerry Chinn while you were in college?

Sure did.

Brad interrupted. "While I answered that question, I wondered what Jerry could have done to have the FBI calling about him."

"I'll bet you did." She continued reading:

Are you aware Chinn currently works at Boeing?

Yeah, he started work there right after college.

Has he ever told you what projects he is working on?

No.

That's good. You do not have a right to know. Every project he has been assigned to has been classified. And now Chinn is being vetted for the second highest level of security clearance in the country. One level below the President himself.

Wow. Jerry Chinn? Are you kidding me?

I do not kid. Now, how well did you know Chinn in college?

We shared quite a few classes.

Did you ever know him to cheat?

No, Jerry was too smart. He didn't need to cheat to get passing grades.

You're right. He is smart. That was a test question to make sure you are telling me the truth. Did you ever socialize with him?

Sure. We went out for pizza and beer or played pool several times.

On those occasions, did he ever once consume alcohol to excess?

No.

Brad interrupted again. "I thought a slight stretching of the truth wouldn't hurt."

Kim smiled with understanding and went on.

Did you ever see him attempting to make covert contact with individuals who might be foreign nationals?

No, I don't think so.

Brad said, "I wondered at the time what the question meant but I was sure the answer should be no."

Did you know he has relatives in Hong Kong?

Yes.

Brad said, "Everyone knew this about Jerry. His favorite sweatshirt in college was one reading, 'Hong Kong Rugby Team,' sent to him by his uncle. I decided this must be another test question."

Good. You are doing well so far. Do you know if Chinn's relatives in Hong Kong ever communicate coded directives to him?

Not to my knowledge.

Do you think a foreign government could bribe Chinn to do their bidding?

No, absolutely not. Jerry has the highest moral standards.

What if they offered him $1 million?

No.

$10 million?

No.

Thank you. You have been most helpful. Do not ever tell anyone we spoke.

Kim looked up after finishing the page and Brad continued. "And then he hung up. At the time, I wondered what had just happened. Now I realize how much I probably contributed to Jerry's career. Since the FBI agent told me never to talk about it, I haven't. I'd like to tell Jerry. It shouldn't matter at this point."

Kim could tell her husband was proud he had been consulted by the FBI. She decided to tease him a little.

"Do you think that you have ever been vetted by the FBI?"

"No. I don't have any secrets anyone would want to know."

"I'm not sure that is the case. They called me a few years ago and asked for a personal reference for you."

"Wow! Really? Whose name did you give them?"

"Jerry Chinn's, of course."

"That is really cool. Why do you think they wanted to know about me?"

"Because you associate closely with someone who has security clearance equal to Jerry's, and they needed to be sure you could be trusted."

"Who could that be?"

"Your wife."

"You? Why would that be? You work at Microsoft."

"I can't tell you. It's classified."

Chapter 28

Bob parked his unmarked Seattle police car in a space marked "Visitor" at the Boeing Renton plant. He turned off the ignition and thought about his impending visit with Jerry Chinn. He had known Jerry in college only as an acquaintance through Brad. Bob had not shared any classes with Jerry because his own degree was in sociology, and he was not required to take many natural science courses. He did remember Jerry as an expert at the game of pool. When the three of them had gone out to play pool and drink beer, Jerry never had to buy the beer. It seemed to Bob he recalled Jerry saying something about having a regulation billiards table in his basement while growing up.

He wondered if Jerry would even remember him, as their paths had not crossed since graduation from college twenty-five years earlier. He knew he would recognize Jerry because he saw his picture in the *Seattle Times* newspaper business section about once every five years. Jerry's bid to take over the low-rent apartment market in the Renton area had not gone unnoticed.

Jerry sat at his desk, stared at his desktop computer screen and tried to look busy when the intercom rang. It was the secretary for his work group announcing a Seattle police detective was there to see him. Jerry quickly closed the solitaire game on his computer and asked, "Does he have an appointment, Susie?"

"No one has an appointment in your schedule. It is wide open for weeks."

"That's because I need to maintain maximum flexibility in case an urgent issue should arise."

"And when did that last happen?"

"I'm not at liberty to tell you. I have the second highest—"

"—level of security clearance available in the United States. I know, I know. You have told me that a million times. I still never see you doing any work. Anyway, what should I tell the detective?"

"Tell him I am very busy today but will try to see him briefly when my current high-level conference ends. He should have scheduled an appointment."

"That would be a first," said Susie, in a low voice.

Jerry spent the next twenty minutes thinking about his apartment rental business, whether he was going anything illegal, and what the detective could want with him. After he had let the enough time pass, he opened his door and Bob walked into the room.

"Hey, I know you!" said Jerry when he saw the man. "UW, sociology major, name is Bob, a friend of Brad Franklin's, and a terrible pool player."

"I'm impressed," said Bob, as the two shook hands. "And I wondered whether you would even recognize me."

"I have a good memory. What are you doing here, anyway? You're not investigating my business activities, are you? My lawyer assures me everything is fully legal."

"No, I'm investigating something else and came to see if you could offer any insight on a couple of things."

"Do I get paid?"

"No, you don't get paid. I just want you to grant a favor to an old acquaintance and let me ask you some questions."

"Nothing lost by asking, I always say."

"What do you know about duct tape?"

"Duct tape? It's stuff you buy at Home Depot and carry around in your car in case you need to fix something. Didn't you take auto shop in high school?"

"Of course I did. That's not the kind of duct tape I'm talking about. I'm talking about Boeing duct tape. Four-hundred-mile-per-hour duct tape."

"Oh, the good stuff. What about it?"

"How easy is it for an employee to get their hands on it?"

"Well, that depends. When it is being used on a project here at Boeing, it is very difficult to access. It is extremely expensive, and the project plans indicate how much is used for every application. If a roll was missing, it would be noticed within a day."

"Have you heard reports of any missing or being stolen? I have two crime scenes where four-hundred-mile-per-hour duct tape was found. Since it is so difficult to access, my pool of candidates who might have some in their possession should be limited. Right?"

"No."

"What do you mean?"

"When a project is over, Boeing disposes of unused consumables like duct tape through the Boeing surplus store. Right now, you can get four-hundred-mile-per-hour there. I go there to look for bargains every day during my break and saw it just yesterday. I have about ten rolls in the back of my pickup truck as we speak. Anyone can shop there."

"Why don't they save it for the next project needing it?"

"Because it would be wasteful. You have to understand, we use the Toyota Production System as our management tool here at Boeing. In TPS, storage space is waste. So they sell it for a dollar a roll."

"And buy more for two hundred dollars a roll when they need some?"

"You've got it! That's what we call reducing waste. It's the same reason my desk has nothing on it. Other papers or folders might interfere with my work when I have an urgent assignment."

"Interesting system. So, anyone in the Puget Sound region could have bought this high-test duct tape at Boeing Surplus?"

"Yep. Just about everyone checking out yesterday had a roll in their basket."

"That doesn't limit things much for me."

Bob continued Jerry's interview. "How about Hong Kong? What do you know about it?"

"Everything."

"Ever been there?"

"Six times. Want to know the years?"

"No, not really. Do you know anything about the use of charcoal in Hong Kong to commit suicide?"

"Sure. I've read all about it. Charcoal suicide is committed by burning charcoal in a small, enclosed room. Burning charcoal produces a huge amount of carbon monoxide, which binds to the hemoglobin in your red blood cells and prevents them from carrying oxygen to tissues like your brain. It is seen as a relatively clean and easy way to commit suicide compared to something like driving your car into a freeway overpass support or cutting yourself with a knife."

"Go on."

"In 1998, a middle-aged woman in Hong Kong with a background in chemical engineering committed charcoal suicide in her small bedroom. The episode was widely publicized in the media and subsequently copied throughout Hong Kong. Within one year, the incidence of charcoal burning suicide in Hong Kong increased six-fold. By 2001, it was the second most common method of suicide in Hong Kong. The method spread like wildfire, so to speak, throughout East Asia to China, Taiwan, and Japan."

"Why did it spread so rapidly?"

"A couple of reasons. One was the media exposure. The press repeatedly called this a painless way to commit suicide. Second is the fact charcoal is readily available to almost everyone. Some government efforts to control the activity have included restrictions on media reporting about suicide and a push toward electric grills while simultaneously making access to charcoal more difficult."

"So what you are telling me, is anyone from Hong Kong and maybe the Far East would know about charcoal and the high amount of carbon monoxide it produces?"

"Yep."

"I came here looking for a Boeing employee with ties to Hong Kong. I'm leaving here looking for someone who might have been to Boeing Surplus at some unknown time and might have knowledge about charcoal. Wow."

Jerry smiled. "Let me know if I can help further. It's been great seeing you but I need to cut things off at this point. My agenda is quite full today."

"Thanks, Jerry. You have been helpful."

Chapter 29

Cathy stuck her head in the doorway of Brad's office and interrupted his work on the computer. "Boss, the King County Medical Examiner's office is on the line holding for you. They said you asked them to call."

"Yeah, I did. Great. Transfer the call, please."

"You got it."

His desk phone rang. "Hello, this is Dr. Franklin. Thanks for calling me."

"Sure. This is Rich McKinsey, Assistant County Medical Examiner. What can I do for you?"

"Did you examine two bodies found yesterday in a warehouse?"

"Yes, I did. Do you know something about them?"

"Oh, sorry. The Seattle Police called me about them yesterday morning. It sounded like they could have died from carbon monoxide poisoning. Do you have preliminary causes of death yet?"

"We do and you are right. Acute carbon monoxide poisoning for both. How did you know?"

"I heard they were cherry red."

"Well, you heard correctly. Both their skin and internal organs. Initial blood carbon monoxide levels were 72% and 78%."

"Those are high enough to kill someone. And fast. Anything else apparent?"

"No, nothing. There is one strange thing, though. The only source of combustion in the room where they died was the natural gas burner in their coffee roaster. The firefighters said it appeared to be functioning normally. We don't often see carbon monoxide fatalities from natural gas appliances."

Brad instantly knew the explanation for the apparent inconsistency. "You're right. Natural gas burns relatively cleanly, particularly when the burner is properly adjusted and the flame is blue, not yellow or orange. A small amount of carbon monoxide is still produced, but usually not enough to cause problems. That's why people can cook with gas stove tops in their kitchens."

He continued, "But there was another source of carbon monoxide in the room. The coffee beans. Unroasted beans are often known as 'coffee cherries' because of their resemblance to the fruit grown in Yakima and made into pies. When a coffee plant's cherries turn from green to red, they are ripe and ready for harvest. I don't know which kind of cherry was the origin for the term cherry red in carbon monoxide poisoning—the fruit or the ripe coffee bean. Both of them are about the same color."

While Brad shared his expertise with the pathologist, he searched the medical articles stored on his hard drive, looking for one about coffee bean carbon monoxide poisoning to e-mail when they finished.

"Unroasted beans are put into a roaster and slowly heated from room temperature to 385°F. This removes all the moisture. The different degrees of roasting are then achieved by reaching various temperatures from 385°F to 435°F, beyond which they will combust. In essence, coffee beans are smoldered, causing them to emit carbon monoxide. Smoldering is the type of burning producing the most carbon monoxide. Just like when charcoal briquettes burn. Dark roast coffee refers to the color of the beans and is reached between 393°F and 435°F. The roasted beans also have small spaces inside them, much like a sponge, filled with carbon monoxide. It is released when the roasted beans are ground."

Rich whistled softly. "That's incredible."

"Yes, it is a little known piece of carbon monoxide trivia. There have been a few case reports of roasters becoming severely poisoned or even dying from carbon monoxide when they have climbed into large coffee bean roasting tanks to clean them. I'd guess the sources of carbon monoxide in the warehouse room, in order of significance, was bean roasting, bean grinding, and then the natural gas burner. Hardly anyone would know about such things."

While he talked, Brad had pulled up the database of cases of carbon monoxide poisoning treated in the department since 1969. He sorted it by "Source of Carbon Monoxide" and asked, "How many charcoal carbon monoxide poisoning deaths do you guys see?"

McKinsey glanced at the wall chart summarizing causes of deaths determined by the department over the preceding twelve months. "Not many. We see a few accidental cases after major winter storms cause power outages and unsuspecting people bring charcoal grills indoors for heat or cooking. But that has really dropped off since the warning label on bags of charcoal was revised a few years ago. Now, most of our charcoal carbon monoxide deaths are suicides by recent immigrants from Asia. Mostly residents of the International District."

"Is there anything in the forensic pathology literature about killing another person by burning charcoal?"

"No, I've never heard of it. And I think I would remember something so unusual."

Brad jotted a note to himself on his desk notepad. "Dr. McKinsey, it has been a pleasure to talk to you."

Chapter 30

B rad walked to the office next door and was glad to see Charles James working at his desk. "Hi, Chuck. Nice to see you. It's been quiet without you for the past weeks. Did you go somewhere interesting?"

"As a matter of fact, I just got back from a dive trip in Mexico."

In addition to being a national expert in chronic wound healing, Charles was well-known in diving circles around the world for his underwater photography. He loved to go on trips to exotic locations in an attempt to get the one underwater shot to top his last one. Many of his photos had graced the covers of magazines such as *SCUBA Diving* and *SCUBA Diver*. His thirst for great pictures required him to pour thousands of dollars annually into dive trips and underwater photographic equipment. But getting another magazine cover was an irresistible lure for him.

"My dive trip started with an eighteen-hour boat trip from Ensenada to the dive site on Guadalupe Island. It was remote, to say the least. The cool thing is that the Mexican government has designated the waters around the island as an ecological biosphere. No one is allowed to put anything into the water that doesn't come back out. Once we got there, about half the people on the boat were seasick and vomiting over the side of the boat. I guess they broke the rule. Those of us who weren't sick got to go down in a shark cage after they did some additional chumming with ground fish. In no time, we had great whites on the scene. I got some great shots. While I was down in a cage at a depth of about fifteen feet, a huge shark rammed the cage and broke a few of the bars. It got my regulator hose in its teeth and ripped it right off. Really exciting!"

"That does sound like a lot of fun." Brad thought how seasick he probably would have been. "What happened then?"

"I held my breath and shot pictures like crazy. Then the crew topside saw what had happened and started to winch me up full speed. The shark pulled his head out, and it took my total concentration to exhale slowly during the ascent so I wouldn't embolize. It was a fantastic trip. I'm going there again next year. I already put down my deposit."

"I'm glad you made it back in one piece. If you are ready to get back to work, I'd like to bounce two cases off you and see what you think."

"If you see me here, I'm ready to work."

"Remember a couple months ago when I told you about the woman who appeared to have attempted suicide by carbon monoxide with her car in the garage but everything didn't fit together?"

"Sure do. I said it might be *murder.* Whatever happened?"

"Well, I got a Seattle police detective involved and it appears it was indeed attempted murder. It looks like someone duct-taped her garage door from the inside, then filled her garage with carbon monoxide by burning charcoal in there."

"The carbon monoxide wasn't from her car?"

"No, her car was brand new and checked out fine. The carbon monoxide appears to have come from some charcoal briquettes."

"And the police have no leads?"

"Well, they might. You are going to hear on the news tonight about two young men who were found dead this morning, apparently while roasting and grinding coffee beans in a small room. The preliminary cause of death is carbon monoxide poisoning."

"Didn't they know enough to ventilate the place?"

"Oh, they did. There was a perfectly adequate ventilation hood running when they were found. But the exhaust duct had been sealed from the outside."

"Do you mean intentionally?"

"Looks like it. With duct tape."

"Wow! Did they know the poisoned female patient?"

"I don't know. We'll have to ask her. This was very special duct tape. Only used in the aerospace industry."

"Has anyone talked to Boeing?"

"The detective is down at the Boeing Renton plant talking to a friend of mine right now."

"This has to be someone with a high level of sophistication about carbon monoxide poisoning. I only know about coffee bean carbon monoxide poisoning because you shared some case report you found in some obscure journal with the docs."

"Yeah, I know. Unfortunately, I made a slide about it and have had it in my standard lecture on carbon monoxide poisoning for about a year. I don't remember how many times I mentioned it or where. Because of that, I'm afraid it narrows the field only about as much as knowing that the duct tape probably came from Boeing. Do you have any ideas?"

"Not off the top of my head. Why don't you discuss it at the meeting of the Metro hyperbaric docs next week and see if anyone has any thoughts? You could also talk about it at the next quarterly hyperbaric staff meeting. There are a bunch of sharp minds on the staff who work all over the city. It may ring a bell for someone."

"Good ideas. Thanks for your help. And I want to see those shark pictures sometime."

Chapter 31

The Seattle weather had indeed changed, even though it was only a week into November. The skies were overcast with low clouds on most days, and there was a seemingly constant mist or steady drizzle falling from the skies. Drivers were continually deciding between having their cars' windshield wipers on or off. Coupled with Seattle's northern latitude, days grew shorter and the time of year approached where those working a full day sometimes went to work in the dark and went home in the dark.

The hyperbaric crew had just finished the last of Friday's four routine treatments, helped the patients change from scrubs back into their street clothes, and ushered them to waiting family members to go home. It was time for the staff to go home, as well, and even though they had punched out on the time clock, Patti, Randy, Carole, and Claude sat in the chamber area. None wanted to head out into the drizzle and face the terrible Friday afternoon traffic.

Randy described his upcoming plans for a trip to San Francisco to visit his brother, Jason, for Thanksgiving.

"Jason and his wife live in Sunnyvale, where I grew up, and both work for Google."

Randy talked with excitement about their stimulating jobs, and how they invited him for Thanksgiving every year, since he was single.

"I fully anticipate the annual lecture from my sister-in-law about how I need to get married. She'll tell me how many single girlfriends she has and if I would only move back to California, she could set me up. I've given up explaining how happy I am in my current position and how much I love living in Seattle. I consider the lecture a 'Thanksgiving tradition.'"

He winked at the group.

Patti spoke up. "Well, I have a long heritage of Thanksgiving traditions better than that. I grew up in Louisiana and the biggest tradition on Thanksgiving Day in New Orleans is eating good food and lots of it! Deep-fried turkey, oyster stuffing, barbequed shrimp, pecan pies—yum! It makes me hungry just to think about it. Of course, it's too far from Seattle for just a holiday trip so my husband, Donald, and I do our best to replicate it here."

"Wait a minute," interrupted Carole, the vocally vegetarian nurse who was dedicated to healthy food and exercise. "Did you say deep-fried turkey? I can't believe it. I mean, I don't believe meat is healthy for you in the first place, but if you want to eat it, it's up to you. But to soak a turkey in oil sounds terrible! It must be soggy with fat."

"Actually, it isn't. When you drop a turkey into hot oil, it seals the outside and keeps the juices in. The skin is brown and crispy while the meat is incredibly moist. Most people use peanut oil because it has a high flash point. You can heat it to a very high temperature without concern for having it flame up."

Patti continued. "But it takes a lot of peanut oil, and it is relatively expensive. So when I was a kid, everyone in the neighborhood would contribute one gallon of oil and they'd fill a fifty-gallon drum about two-thirds full. A propane burner heated it outdoors, and folks would come by and drop their turkeys in. Because the hot oil is both outside and inside the bird, they cook really fast compared to using an oven. A fifteen-pound turkey takes less than an hour. Donald and I still cook them that way. We have a five-gallon turkey cooker that we fill with oil and power with a propane tank in the backyard. Carole, why don't you come over to our house on Thanksgiving and try it? Maybe we'd convert you to eating meat."

"*That* won't happen. But I will stop by on Thanksgiving because I want to see this. I'll bring something for myself to eat. Probably some tofurkey, turkey-shaped tofu. But I do love pecan pie . . ."

Randy said, "It has never made sense to me why vegetarians like to have their food in the shape of animals or other foods they won't eat, like hot dogs. Strange. What about you, Claude, do you have any childhood

Thanksgiving traditions?"

Claude roused from deep thought. "No, I really don't. As you know, I grew up in Richland near Hanford but didn't have much family around me. My parents both died when I was relatively young, and I don't have any siblings."

"Do you mean the place over in eastern Washington?" asked Carole.

"Yeah. It actually has an interesting history. Hanford was a bustling agricultural community next to the Columbia River until 1943 when the federal government condemned the entire community and gave its residents thirty-day eviction notices. The government then bulldozed the place and built a nuclear production facility known as the Hanford Site. In 1944, there were 45,000 men, including my grandfather, working on construction of the nuclear plant at Hanford. If you can believe it, less than 1% of the workmen knew the purpose was to manufacture the radioactive payload for a nuclear weapon to use to end World War II. Plutonium manufactured at Hanford was used in the nuclear bomb detonated over Nagasaki, Japan. During the Cold War, Hanford expanded to nine nuclear reactors and five plutonium-processing complexes. The facility is said to have provided plutonium for over 60,000 US nuclear weapons. My dad worked there in the sixties. I guess my family's tradition is working at Hanford."

"But why aren't you following the family tradition?"

"The place is a mess now. It turns out early procedures used to dispose of the nuclear waste have been inadequate and unsafe. There is a lot of contaminated water and land. It's not my cup of tea to work in cleaning up radioactive waste."

Claude looked around the group and saw the concerned faces of his co-workers. "It's okay, guys. It's just what happened. I have a Thanksgiving tradition now. Brad knows my situation and the fact I have no family, so he invites me to his home for Thanksgiving every year. I'm good."

An awkward silence prevailed. Everyone still felt guilty about advertising their plans to celebrate the family holiday when Claude didn't even have a family.

Claude clapped his hands together and said, "Let's hit the road. One thing that we can all be thankful for is the traffic should be dissipating now."

Chapter 32

Because more than one-half of the staff in Metropolitan Hospital's hyperbaric department worked per diem and had primary jobs elsewhere, Brad held quarterly meetings for his employees. The purpose was to update staff about new hospital regulations and requirements, updated department policies, and to educate them about hyperbaric medicine. He felt an educated employee who knew why he performed the duties of his job, in addition to how to perform them, provided better patient care. In addition, the more camaraderie he could generate among his crew, the better they worked as a team.

But he had a different agenda for this afternoon's gathering.

Claude had just finished his PowerPoint presentation on the value of checklists in medicine. He had been assigned the duty when he was caught showing off his pet geoduck clam to the attractive EMT crew leader instead of doing his job three months earlier.

Brad stood up. "Claude, your talk was fantastic. You hit every important point like a hammer hitting the heads of a row of nails. When Atul Gawande published his book, *The Checklist Manifest: How to Get Things Right* back in 2009, he opened a lot of eyes. He pointed out there are two kinds of errors people make. First are errors of ignorance, or mistakes we make because we don't have enough knowledge. Second are errors of ineptitude, or mistakes we make because we don't properly use the information we do know.

"In modern society, most failure results from the latter. This is especially true in medicine. There is no shortage of medical knowledge, that's for sure. There is so much information at our fingertips online, people practicing medicine make mistakes doing things which appear to be routine because they can't possibly juggle all the information available."

Brad walked to the front of the conference room. "Medicine adopted the use of checklists from industries where a worker missing a step can be catastrophic, like airline pilots and people who build skyscrapers. No one should be embarrassed to use a checklist. It is not an admission you don't know enough. Think of it as an admission you know too much. You are an expert.

"As Claude just told us, there have been numerous studies in the medical field demonstrating checklists improve the quality and consistency of patient care, and sometimes save lives. Recently, a group in Scandinavia performed a systematic review of those studies. They found checklists in medicine improved communication, reduced adverse events, improved adherence with guidelines, and also reduced morbidity and mortality. No study published to date shows decreased patient safety or quality after introducing checklists in medicine. Claude did a great job summarizing the information. I am going to talk to the Director of Medical Education here at Metro and see if I can get Claude on the schedule to give his presentation to the weekly combined house-staff conference. There are a lot of residents who could learn something from Claude."

During Brad's accolades, Claude had found his way to a chair in the corner of the conference room. When he finished his comments, Claude responded, "Thanks, Brad. But remember why I was given the 'opportunity' to give this presentation. Because I was goofing off and not doing my tasks on the critical care checklist."

Brad smiled. "I suspect it won't happen again, will it?"

Claude smiled back and replied, "Not likely, Boss."

Brad focused his attention back to the group. "I have another issue I'd like to run past you guys. The Seattle Police and I need some help solving a crime. Any ideas you have are welcome. I'll try to summarize briefly. Some of you will remember we treated a young woman named Laurie Rodgers for what appeared at the time to be intentional carbon monoxide poisoning. It turns out someone was trying to injure her, at the very least. The carbon monoxide in her garage was not from her vehicle but from some charcoal briquettes which were burned inside before she entered. Whoever put the burning charcoal in the garage also sealed the door with duct tape."

The staff looked at each other. It wasn't often their boss came to them for advice.

"You have undoubtedly heard news reports about the two young men who died recently while roasting coffee in an old warehouse. The media ascribed it to 'the accumulation of fumes' from the gas roaster. They weren't aware these two were experienced roasters who had installed adequate ventilation equipment. The reason the carbon monoxide built up was someone had used duct tape to seal closed the ventilation duct vent."

Claude spoke up. "You know, I think Randy and I may have seen those guys at a bar. What do you think, Randy?"

Randy looked up from texting on his phone and responded, "The guys we met were setting up a coffee company near Boeing field. Where were these two found?"

"I don't know where the warehouse was. But I am in touch with the detective on the case and will find out. If it was in the same area, he may want to talk to the both of you."

"The Seattle Police are involved?" asked Earl. "Do they think both events are related?"

"That's what it looks like," replied Brad.

Carole built on Earl's thought, "This would have to be someone who knows a heck of a lot about carbon monoxide poisoning. There probably aren't a lot of people outside of hyperbaric medicine who understand how much carbon monoxide is produced by both charcoal burning and coffee bean roasting."

Randy asked, "Does the fact duct tape used in both instances give any clues to the perpetrator? I mean who uses duct tape, anyway? Furnace installers?"

"Good question. I've learned more about duct tape in the last couple of months than I ever believed possible. It turns out everyone uses it, except apparently you and me, to repair just about everything. This was unusual duct tape, a type used in the aerospace industry. The Seattle Police believe it probably came from Boeing Surplus."

Patti added her thoughts. "These people can't have been poisoned at random. The events sound very planned. If you ask me, you need to figure out what the victims had in common. Sure, the murderer knows a lot about carbon monoxide. But people other than those of us in this room do also. Was Laurie connected to the two dead guys in any way?"

"You have identified the question of the day right now, Patti. I'll talk to the detective on the case. I'm sure he is investigating connections between the victims, but I'll re-emphasize it."

Brad picked up his notes and prepared to leave.

"It's time for us to get out of here. Thanks for spending some extra time and brainstorming, you guys. Once this is solved, I plan to nominate you for Metro's Outstanding Team Award. You deserve it."

The staff members walked out smiling, proud of the recognition that nomination for the coveted award would bring, but even more excited about the bonuses that would accompany it if they won.

Chapter 33

The cell phone rang during dinner. The rule in the Franklin household was no one would interrupt the dinner hour to answer a phone. Dinner was a family affair and a time for parents and children alike to share the events of their day. The only exception was when Brad was on call for hyperbaric, which he was that night. As he reached over and picked up the ringing phone from the kitchen counter, Ann and Lynn exchanged knowing glances with their mother. Dad was probably going back to work tonight.

"This is Dr. Brad Franklin," he answered.

The Metropolitan Hospital operator responded. "Dr. Franklin, I have Dr. Michael from County Medical Center Emergency Department holding for you. Are you able to take the call?"

Feeling guilty as his family sat patiently and waited for him to get off the phone, he replied, "Sure. Put him through."

"Hello? Dr. Michael, how can I help you?"

"Dr. Franklin, I apologize profusely for bothering you at this hour of the day, but I have two patients who may need your services. I'd like to tell you about them and get your advice."

"Go on."

"The patients are Mr. John Drinkwater and his wife, Essie. Do you recognize the name?"

"Sure. It would be hard not to. During the election two weeks ago, John Drinkwater was all over the news campaigning against Washington State Initiative 1069. He did not want the state to place a ban on the use of Styrofoam for food packaging, claiming it would hurt the economy. It was hard to buy his argument in a state with an economy helped by every tree grown."

"He's the one. John and Essie came home from having cocktails at the Rainier Club happy hour this evening about 6:00 p.m. We know because the valet delivered their car to them at 5:45 and it only about fifteen minutes from the club to their home in Madison Park. Friends from the club stopped by about 6:30 to take them to dinner at Canlis Restaurant on Queene Anne Hill. They rang the bell and knocked on the door but no one answered. The friends tried the door and it was unlocked. They walked inside and found the Drinkwaters unconscious on their bedroom floor. They were only half-clothed and appeared to have been changing for dinner.

"According to a neighbor walking his dog past the house, the friends came running out the front door, screaming for someone to call 9-1-1. The dog walker called on his cell phone and Medic-1 was on scene in two minutes. They found Mr. Drinkwater in ventricular fibrillation, shocked him out of it into sinus tachycardia, and intubated him. Mrs. Drinkwater had a pulse but was in impending respiratory arrest so the medics intubated her for airway protection during transfer. We have them in the County Emergency Department now."

"And you are calling me because . . . ?"

"They have carbon monoxide poisoning. Arterial blood laboratory testing on Mr. Drinkwater shows a severe metabolic acidosis with pH 7.15, PCO_2 30 and carbon monoxide level 48%. Mrs. Drinkwater's numbers aren't as bad, with pH 7.30, PCO_2 35 and carbon monoxide 40%. I am calling to inquire whether we should transfer them to Metro for hyperbaric treatment?"

"What was the evidence John Drinkwater was in V-fib?"

"The Medic-1 medics transmitted the tracing from their defibrillator to County triage. I saw it myself and can confirm it."

"Then he has an incredibly poor prognosis. We have never treated a carbon monoxide poisoned patient with documented associated cardiac arrest who did not eventually die. It seems the severity of the carbon monoxide poisoning in association with the no blood flow state from the cardiac arrest may be an unsurvivable insult. In most cases, they are treated emergently in the hyperbaric chamber, admitted afterward to the ICU, and diagnosed with brain death. The ICU team ends up withdrawing life support after two to three days."

"So we shouldn't treat him?"

"I probably wouldn't if it involved long-distance transport or if he was the only one poisoned. However, his wife is definitely a candidate for hyperbaric oxygen, and we can treat both of them simultaneously on the remote chance we might help him. Please arrange for their transport to the Metropolitan Emergency Department. While you are waiting for two ambulances with advanced cardiac life support capability transport to be set up, please ask your resident to place an arterial line in each of them. We'll use it for pressure monitoring and arterial blood gas monitoring during treatment."

"Thanks so much for your help."

"I'll be on my way to Metro in a few minutes and will meet them in the ED when they arrive."

Brad disconnected the call and looked at his daughters. "Dad is going back to work." They nodded knowingly. But before he could get up from the table, fourteen-year-old Ann spoke up.

"Dad, can you translate what you just said on the phone into regular English so we can understand why you need to go back to work tonight?"

Brad smiled at his wife. "Sure, sweetie. I have to be somewhat careful with what I tell any of you because there are laws against revealing a person's private health information. But this will be on the news at 11:00 tonight and be public information by that time, I'm sure."

Brad scooted his chair in between those of his daughters.

"The call was from Dr. Michael in the Emergency Room at County General Hospital. They have a husband and wife there with severe carbon monoxide poisoning. Some friends came to pick them up this evening to go out to dinner and found them unconscious. We need to treat them in the hyperbaric chamber as soon as possible to clear the carbon monoxide from their bodies so they can hopefully recover. Unfortunately, one of them had a bad type of heart attack from the poisoning and probably won't survive even with the hyperbaric oxygen."

"Where did the carbon monoxide come from?"

"I don't know. Since this is the time of year when cold weather makes people start using their furnaces again, it's probably a faulty furnace."

"Is that why the furnace guy was at our house last week?"

"It sure is. Everyone needs to get their furnace checked once a year but lots of people don't do it. Our furnace checked out fine. Don't worry. You'll be okay."

He then turned his attention to Kim. "Sorry I won't be able to watch a movie on Netflix with you tonight. I'll be home around eleven, if all goes smoothly."

"Go do your job. I may not wait up for you. I know from experience your estimates of time are always optimistic."

Brad smiled, walked around the table giving each of them a hug, and headed out the kitchen door to the garage.

Chapter 34

Before starting the family Prius, Brad called the hyperbaric charge nurse on call for the night. Patti answered on the second ring.

"What do we have, Boss?"

"Two comatose and intubated patients with carbon monoxide poisoning are being transferred from County for hyperbaric treatment. They are husband and wife, approximate age sixty years. They sound hemodynamically stable now, but the male was initially found in V-fib arrest in the field."

"Ouch. Bad sign. How did they get poisoned? House fire?"

"No, it wasn't a fire. They were found down in their bedroom in Madison Park. Playing the odds at this time of year, it was probably a furnace accident. This happened within the hour, so I am sure the Seattle Fire Department is still checking things out. We'll need to treat them both on ventilators simultaneously, so we'll do one in Port Lock and one in Starboard Lock. We'll need an inside attendant for each. I'd like to open the doors between the locks so we can operate the whole system as one chamber. That way, the inside attendants can help each other out. But because of the possibility some event could necessitate separation of the locks, we should have a second chamber operator onsite."

"Got it. I'll have everyone there and ready to go in thirty minutes."

Chapter 35

By the time he arrived, Patti, inside attendants Dawna and Carole, as well as chamber operator Randy were waiting.

"Hi guys. Thanks for coming in tonight. Patti, I know we only have one operator on call. Were you able to find another one?"

"I called around without success, then called Claude. He's willing to operate tonight, if needed, since today is Wednesday and he was off to teach scuba. He is on his way in from home."

"Great. We're set. I came in through the ED and saw the patients being unloaded from the transport rigs. Both intubated, as billed. I took a look at the chest x-rays sent with them from County, and they looked fine. Also, both have arterial lines. Dr. Michael at County Hospital was most helpful, as usual."

Claude walked in a few minutes later, just as the

patients were being rolled on stretchers through the back entrance. "Hi everybody. I'm here and the first thing I am going to do is exchange the air in the endotracheal tube cuffs for saline."

Brad nodded in appreciation. "Yet another success story for checklists in medicine. You folks know your jobs. Let's get these patients in the chamber and get them started as soon as we can."

The crew busied themselves with the tasks at hand, got the patients into the chamber with ventilators set up, arterial lines calibrated, and cardiac monitoring online in less than ten minutes.

Patti announced, "Ready to pressurize, Brad."

"Good work, guys. We'll treat on our usual U.S. Air Force table at sixty-six feet of seawater maximum pressure. Randy, you're operating all three locks as one chamber. It's going to take a lot of air to get the whole complex to sixty-six feet. Claude, will you keep a close eye on the volume tank pressures and compressor bank?"

"Sure. But it will go just fine. I have done after-hours simulations a number of times and we have enough gas in those tanks to take the whole thing to 165 feet. This will be a piece of cake."

Chapter 36

Claude was right. The chamber pressurization went without incident. Soon, arterial blood gases had been checked at depth, ventilators adjusted, arterial line calibration confirmed, and intravenous fluids adjusted. Dawna and Carole settled down in chairs next to their patients within the chamber, hoping for an uneventful subsequent two hours.

Brad spoke to Randy, Patti, and Claude outside the chamber. "I did not mention it until now because I didn't want anything to slow us down, but our male patient is something of a celebrity. Does anyone recognize him?"

The three shook their heads.

"John Drinkwater is a local businessman who was all over the news earlier this month before the election. He was very outspoken in opposition to the statewide initiative to ban Styrofoam packaging in Washington. Many think his comments about it hurting the economy singlehandedly defeated the initiative."

Randy commented, "Oh, I remember him now. I never could understand his logic since we have no Styrofoam manufacturing in Washington and a ban would only seem to help our timber industry, since most Styrofoam replacements are paper-based."

Patti asked, "Why does everyone want to replace Styrofoam anyway? I think it's great stuff. It keeps take-out food hot, protects eggs on the way home from the grocery store, and the peanuts are used to pack everything."

Claude looked at Randy. "Do you want to start or should I?"

"I'll lead off," replied Randy.

"Okay, Patti, listen up. Styrofoam is the brand name for polystyrene foam. Polystyrene foam is a lightweight product, comprised of about 95% air. You are right. It has very good insulating and cushioning properties. It is used widely for product packaging and shipping applications. Those are the good things about Styrofoam."

"What are the bad things?"

"Polystyrene foam has not been shown to degrade or break down over time. Because of this, it is a major environmental concern. Landfills in the US are estimated to comprise approximately 30% polystyrene foam by volume. No one knows how long it may take polystyrene foam to biodegrade but some experts have estimated over five hundred years."

Claude built upon Randy's explanation. "And we use a lot of it. It has been estimated Americans throw away over twenty-five billion Styrofoam cups annually. Enough Styrofoam cups are produced daily to circle the Earth if they were lined up end-to-end."

"Can't it be recycled?"

"It can be, but it is not cost-effective because the volume is so great for the amount of polystyrene recovered."

"In addition to filling up landfills, it chokes birds and other animals."

"So what can we do about it?"

"Rather than recycling polystyrene foam, we should be pre-cycling it. The solution to the Styrofoam problem is finding and using alternative materials so Styrofoam is not manufactured in the first place. Recycled paper products are probably the best alternative. Paper is recyclable, biodegradable, and nontoxic to the environment. Trees are a renewable resource."

"Then why was Mr. Drinkwater so opposed to a Styrofoam ban in Washington?"

Brad broke into the discussion. "I can answer that one. Yesterday, it was publically revealed his company, Drinkwater Industries, not only manufactures cardboard shipping boxes here in Washington State but also has a subsidiary in Indiana which is the second largest producer of Styrofoam peanuts in the country. Some investigative reporters from one of the local television stations figured out the connection and broke the story on the news last night."

Randy responded. "I heard the story on the radio this morning. It really irritated me. The economy the guy was talking about was his own, not the state's. He would continue to sell cardboard boxes whether the state bans Styrofoam or not. The only risk for him was having our state stop buying his Indiana Styrofoam products. He was lying in order to keep his pocketbook lined."

Brad immediately replied, "Whoa! We will have no talk like that about our patients in this department. Do you understand, Randy?"

"Yes, sir."

Over the next few days, things played out for John Drinkwater as Brad had predicted. He remained in a dense coma after three hyperbaric treatments. The consulting neurologist ordered a brain blood flow scan and an EEG. The scan showed no blood flow into the skull because the brain was so swollen. The EEG showed no brain wave activity. He was pronounced brain-dead.

The Drinkwaters' son flew in from Chicago. He ran the Indiana Styrofoam subsidiary from an office there, where the media had speculated he liked the Windy City better than a rural town in southern Indiana. In addition, it was easier for the privately held family business to be able to make ecological claims in Washington State if the corporate connection was as unclear as possible.

Once the son was on site, he was allowed time with his father and then life support was withdrawn.

Mrs. Drinkwater fared better. By the morning following her first hyperbaric treatment, she was awake but confused. She received two additional treatments on the day following her poisoning and slowly improved. At the time of her discharge to a neurorehabilitation center one week later, she was ambulatory but still suffering severe memory loss. It was unclear whether she understood the fact her husband had died. Their son was very busy getting both of his parents' affairs in order, coordinating his mother's placement, and attempting to keep the company running smoothly. The media was constantly badgering him with questions about the Styrofoam production facility and the accusations concerning his father's concealment when campaigning against the Styrofoam ban.

He was unable to provide any explanations for them.

Chapter 37

Brad asked Cathy to arrange a meeting between Claude, Earl, and himself at Lowell's Restaurant in the Pike Place Market Saturday at nine in the morning, when none of them were scheduled to be work. Breakfast would be his treat. He knew both would show up for the opportunity.

The Pike Place Market was perhaps the most well-known landmark in Seattle, outside of the Space Needle. It was certainly the most popular tourist attraction. The Market in downtown Seattle perched on a hill overlooking the Elliott Bay Waterfront. Condominiums in the neighborhood, with the same view, commanded very high prices.

The Market was founded in 1907. It was one of the longest continuously operating farmer's markets in the United States. The Market was an outlet for many small farmers, craftspeople, florists, and fishmongers, as well as the location for a number of restaurants.

Some of the eateries were longstanding, low-profile, and known best to natives. Among these was Lowell's, self-described as "almost classy" since it was founded in 1957 and home of some of the best view tables in the city. Breakfast at Lowell's was especially popular. Guests placed their order at the counter, then wandered up a stairway to find a table on one of the three floors above, all with windows from floor to ceiling and expansive views of Elliot Bay. Lingering over a long weekend breakfast at Lowell's watching the super ferries ply their way across the Sound was an experience true Northwesterners savored.

Brad stood in the Pike Place Market near the counter at Lowell's, pondering the menu on the wall. Northwest Dungeness crab eggs Benedict included two poached eggs on rosemary toast topped with heaps of Dungeness crabmeat and drowned in Hollandaise sauce. Hash browns came on the side. Smoked fresh king salmon could be substituted for the crab. Still indecisive, he noticed Earl and Claude walking up together.

"Good morning guys! Did you ride the same bus?"

"No, we didn't ride the bus, but we should have. Claude drove us. But the parking around here is terrible! All the spaces on the streets are taken and the parking lots around the Market are outrageous. Every tourist visiting this city must rent a car and then schedule their visit to the Pike Place Market on Saturday morning. We finally found a space in a lot over on Virginia costing only ten bucks for two hours. This is another reason I ride my bike or use public transportation."

"I invited you to breakfast, so I'll pay the parking. You guys know those nice sports stadiums we have? They are some of the many things visitors pay for through taxes on cars rented at SeaTac Airport. So don't begrudge them their need to park around here. Anyway, I suppose you two already know what you are having for breakfast?"

Claude spoke without hesitation. "Hangtown Fry for me every time. I can already taste the bacon, eggs, Pacific oysters, and Parmesan cheese."

He gave them the thumbs-up sign.

"Do you guys know how it got its name and why it was invented? During the California Gold Rush, a miner came into a saloon in what was called Hangtown, now Placerville, and told the bartender he wanted the most expensive breakfast possible because he had just hit it rich. The most expensive ingredients they had were oysters that needed to be brought up from San Francisco before the ice they were packed in melted, eggs that survived the trip without breaking, and bacon. It's a great combination. It's said the miner paid one hundred fifty dollars for breakfast."

Brad looked at the menu on the wall again. "Well, I guess I'm lucky Lowell's only charges seventeen dollars."

"I'll have the San Juan Eggs Benedict," replied Earl. "The one made with half crab and half smoked salmon."

Brad decided against the eggs Benedict and said, "And I love the corned beef hash here. With poached eggs. While I put in our orders, why don't you guys go upstairs and find us a great view table?"

After paying, Brad had to climb to the third level to find his two employees. "You didn't want to make it easy on an old guy, did you?" He sat down in the chair facing the spectacular view.

Earl wanted to know what was going on. "Claude and I have no idea why you invited us out to breakfast and what you want to talk about. Not that we aren't good company, but you do see a lot of us at work."

"I want to talk with you two about a patient the rest of the crew doesn't know and see if you can give me any insight. Do you both remember Floyd Ashton?"

Earl responded, "Yep, sure do. Floyd is the diver who went unconscious and developed pulmonary edema at depth. Because he was middle-aged, it was concluded he must have had a heart attack. He had the dive buddy in the hot pink thong."

"Her name was Candy," said Claude. "As you guys know, I trained both of them. Did something else happen?"

"Yes and no. I got a phone call yesterday from Dr. Steves about the blood samples we sent for his decompression sickness study. His lab tech thought the anticoagulated sample in the green top tube looked a little too bright red for venous blood and ran a carbon monoxide level on it. It turns out the blood could be described as cherry red. The carbon monoxide level was 44%."

"Holy smokes!" exclaimed Earl. "Maybe it's the wrong term to use, but it means Floyd had carbon monoxide poisoning as the explanation for his event. How did he get that?"

Brad watched the food server find the number they had placed on the table and pass out the meals. Only when he walked away did he continue. "Most likely he had contaminated air in his tank. Claude, you trained them. Do you remember anything about his equipment?"

"Yeah, I do. Floyd was flush with cash at the time and bought everything brand new from some online dive shop."

"Where did he get his tank filled? Earl, do you remember Candy told us how they had to make a detour that morning to pick up their tanks which had been dropped off for filling?"

"Yeah, I remember her saying something about it but don't think she said where."

"During the time I was instructing them, I filled their tanks at my place. It's included in the class price," said Claude. "But I didn't do that fill. The simple thing to do is to ask Floyd. You must have brought us out to brainstorm with you because you can't find him."

"Very perceptive. When I got the call yesterday, I immediately called Floyd's phone number listed in his Metro hospital record. It was a cell phone and the number now belongs to someone else. So, I called his apartment complex office. Floyd moved out a while back, but they all remember him because he didn't pay out his one-year lease. I guess his scheme of farming genetically modified salmon was coming under some scrutiny by the University of Washington Fisheries Department. Floyd unloaded his interest at a discount on some unsuspecting soul and headed for Asia to look into shrimp farms. So there is no way to get in touch with him."

"What are you thinking?"

"Floyd's carbon monoxide poisoning could have been accidental or intentional. We've all heard of divers who got a bad air fill from a second-rate shop. It totally explains his episode. With carbon monoxide poisoning, he certainly would have developed alteration of consciousness at depth. And the pulmonary edema could have resulted from impairment of cardiac function by the carbon monoxide. What I'm thinking is if Floyd's poisoning was intentional, it could somehow be related to the others we discussed at the staff meeting. The thing making me suspicious is Candy told us both of their tanks had been filled and yet she had no problems. She probably did not have carbon monoxide in hers."

"Why not just ask Candy where they were filled?" asked Earl.

"It is apparent to me you will need to learn some things before you get married. Candy is an exotic dancer, and I have no idea where she works. My wife would not look kindly upon a proposal from me saying I need to go to all the strip clubs in Seattle to find a dancer named Candy and ask her some questions about diving."

Claude sat up straight in his chair. "I know her better than anyone because I made her acquaintance through dive training. I'm willing to go to all the strip clubs in Seattle to look for her."

Brad shook his head knowingly. "I'll bet you are. I'll see if the detective working our cases needs any help and let you know."

Chapter 38

Bob Heimbigner sat in the department waiting room to greet Brad when he arrived Monday morning.

"We need to talk. Now."

"But I have clinical responsibilities this morning with patients to see and treatments to supervise."

"Can't you find someone else to do it? I really need to talk with you."

"Okay. Let me go down the hall and see if Kurt Stevens is in. I think he is scheduled for administrative time this morning. He owes me some hyperbaric coverage for one time when he has asked me to cover for him because he somehow got double booked. I'll be right back."

Brad returned in five minutes. "We're good. Kurt was there and will cover for me. He's a great guy. He would give the shirt off his back to help you."

"Great. I'll send Dr. Stevens two complimentary tickets to this year's Policemen's Ball. Anyway, a couple

NEIL B. HAMPSON, MD

of weeks ago your team suggested looking for similarities in the victims, something we were already doing. I have found a few things tying them together. In addition, I have evidence Mr. and Mrs. Drinkwater, who you treated, were intentionally poisoned. It was no furnace accident."

"I'm all ears."

"Okay. First, the Drinkwaters. When Seattle Fire extracted them from their home and then inspected it, one of the things they did was to map the house carbon monoxide levels."

"What do you mean?"

"They went into every room, stairway, and hallway in the house and measured carbon monoxide concentrations immediately after getting the victims out. Then they drew a map of the house including furnace ductwork, vents, and the like. The heating duct leading to their bedroom feeds the kitchen and the library first. Heating vents were open in both of those rooms, yet carbon monoxide levels were dramatically lower than the bedroom. The only room with a level higher than the bedroom was a storage room on the second floor.

"At first we thought it was a mistake because there is no physical connection from the storage room to the bedroom. It doesn't even have a heating vent in it. Then one of the fire investigators recalled a recent study presented at the National Fire Protection Association meeting demonstrating carbon monoxide can pass through wallboard."

Brad swiveled in his chair and pulled a book of meeting abstracts from his bookcase.

"That's true. Wallboard is made of gypsum, a porous mineral. Carbon monoxide molecules are so small the pores in gypsum are about one million times their size. It poses virtually no obstruction to carbon monoxide diffusion. As you can see here, that study was also presented at last year's Hyperbaric Medical Society meeting. It solved a mystery for us. Prior to this, we have always explained that patients are poisoned in multiple locations within an apartment building because carbon monoxide travelled through ducts or common spaces like hallways or stairwells. Now we know it's not always the answer. You didn't find another can of charcoal ash in the storeroom, did you, Bob?"

"No, at first we didn't think we had found any source of carbon monoxide. There was a gasoline-powered electrical generator there, but it appeared to be brand new, had no gas in it, and didn't look like it had been used. But again, one of the sharp investigators noticed the ignition switch was in the 'on' position, not the way it would have been shipped from the factory. So they broke it down and found traces of gasoline in the tank and fuel filter. It looks like someone ran it until it ran out of gas, probably to generate the high amount of carbon monoxide in the bedroom."

"Planning this event required some sophistication."

"It sure did. And I put our department profilers onto the issue of what the victims could have in common. They went through every note, record, and piece of evidence. It doesn't appear the victims knew each other, but they did share something in common."

"Really? What's that?"

"None of them were green."

"Are you trying to set me up for a bad joke about cherry red?"

"No, now get serious and listen to me. I mean green as in environmentally conscious. Laurie Rodgers was the first one poisoned, as far as we are aware, right? Well, she is a huge consumer of energy for her transportation. She drives a flashy Cadillac Escalade, solo, to and from work every day. I put it in my report she said to me she didn't care how much gas she used since she was rich and could afford it."

"Hmmm. Interesting theory. What about the coffee bean roasters who died in October?"

"The profilers picked something strange in these evidence reports from the scene. The sample-size vacuum-packed bags they had printed read, 'Seattle Shade Coffee Company. Only shade-grown beans.' But the big bags of beans they were roasting weren't shade-grown. It's possible they were trying to fool people and get them to buy sun-grown beans as ecologically sensitive coffee."

"I'm beginning to see where you are going with this."

Brad reached into his desk drawer, took out a pad of paper and began to write down a list of the incidents.

"Now we know Drinkwater was murdered with carbon monoxide and his ties to Styrofoam production in Indiana have been revealed. He fits the pattern perfectly. What do you think?"

"I think I may have a couple more for you. We didn't know it at the time, but a middle-aged diver named Floyd Ashton came through here in September with a very unusual presentation for a diving accident. We just found out he was poisoned with carbon monoxide while diving. Both he and his dive buddy had their tanks filled at the same time, yet she did fine. It looks like Floyd was targeted when someone put carbon monoxide in his dive tank. Even more, Floyd was as non-green as they come. He bragged about a large amount of money he made taking advantage of an oil spill in the Gulf. Then he moved to Seattle and was in the business not only of raising salmon in pens in the Sound, attendant with all of their pollution, but also using genetically modified fish that might impact the wild strains if they escaped the pens and mated with them."

"So do you know who filled their tanks? They are our suspects!"

"Unfortunately, we don't. Floyd has since skipped the area and is somewhere in Southeast Asia, so we can't ask him. His dive buddy was an exotic dancer named Candice Mays, who went by the name of Candy. But we don't know where she is, either. Maybe your guys could run a search for Candice Mays."

"Yeah, right. Doc, you think too literally. Don't you get it? It is obviously a fictional name. Candice Mays goes by Candy Mays. Mays sounds the same as maize, which is the Native American word for corn. Candice Mays translates to Candy Corn, a delectable Halloween treat, I might add. She probably just uses the name in the weeks before Halloween. We won't find her."

"Wow, no wonder you're a detective. Anyway, the final case which may relate is the family of four we treated last month when they were poisoned in a house fire."

"Are you talking about the Canadian who was building a mega-home on the last undeveloped shoreline on Lake Union? The fire the media was so excited about?"

"You've got it."

"Our profilers had actually picked up on the case and included it in this list until a letter arrived last week at the department. Keep this under your hat because it is still an open case, but the letter was from the Earth Protection Organization, claiming responsibility for the fire. In the letter, they actually apologized for poisoning the family, as human injury was not their intent. They claim not to have known the family was sleeping in the house. But they said they will continue to perform 'nonviolent' acts to protect the Earth, so we are still looking for them."

The two old college friends stared across the desk at each other until Brad spoke. "Do I understand correctly that we are dealing with an eco-terrorist? Someone who hates those who don't care for the Earth?"

"That's exactly what I came to tell you. Your team was right. All the victims have something in common. And now your Mr. Ashton is added to the list. As you might expect, my profilers also provided me with some research on eco-terrorism since this was brought forward. Let me read you a little of their summary.

"Eco-terrorism refers to acts of violence against other people or their property in support of ecological or environmental causes. The FBI defines eco-terrorism as the use of violence against people or property by an environmentally oriented group for environmental or political reasons or aimed at an audience beyond the target."

Brad said, "An environmentally oriented group suggests we are dealing with more than one person."

"Seems like the most likely scenario."

"Also, these victims were committing ecological infractions ranging from wasting fuel to polluting the sea, air, and land."

"Right. No real focus. Some of those labeled as eco-terrorists do not commit violence against humans, only against property owned by large corporations. Much of what they do falls into the category of sabotage, unlike our perpetrator or perpetrators. The thought is eco-terrorism arose from something called radical environmentalism in the 1960s. Radical environmentalism is characterized by the belief human society is responsible for depletion of the environment and if this is left unchecked, complete environmental destruction will occur."

"Do they have any examples in the research you've got?"

"Yeah, they do. One example is tree spiking or driving nails or small spikes into tree trunks to prevent logging. Hitting one with a chainsaw would be a disaster. Another example is arson, which is a common tactic of gangs like the Earth Protection Organization. They burn down housing developments or shopping malls."

"What about individuals killing people in the name of environmentalism, like we are talking about?"

"The most well-known example given in this report is Theodore Kaczynski, better known as the Unabomber. He was a serial murderer who killed three people and injured twenty-three more. He opposed many forms of industrialization and attacked people associated with modern technology by planting or mailing homemade bombs. He was a child genius who got into Harvard at age sixteen. While there, he was one of a group of twenty-two undergraduates who participated as research subjects in a series of experiments which were subsequently determined to be of questionable ethical nature. The experiments were designed to measure an individual's responses to extreme stress. The students were subjected to personally abusive attacks, including assaults to their egos, cherished ideas, and beliefs. Some have speculated Kaczynski's later actions could somehow have been in response to this level of stress."

"Anything more in their profiling report?"

"There is more, but you've heard the executive summary. It would appear we are dealing with eco-terrorism, but we don't know if it is a group or an individual. As long as I continue to make steady progress like this, the Seattle Police Chief is willing to let me have the case. News of the Floyd Ashton incident will help me in that regard. As soon as things start to slow, they are going to call in the FBI. I sure wish we could locate your Candice Mays. She could crack the thing wide open. The boys in vice will be happy to look for her if you can provide a description."

"I can give you one, but it will be sketchy since I only saw her once for about five minutes. Our charge nurse Earl saw her for the same amount of time. He's working in the chamber area this morning. After you talk to Earl, ask him to track down our hyperbaric engineer, Claude. He's a former navy diver who gives recreational scuba lessons. He trained Floyd and Candy, so he should be able to describe her the best. You'll get along well. Claude grew up in the Tri-Cities in eastern Washington, not far from your old stomping grounds."

Chapter 39

Bob sat with Claude in his combination office and engineering shop.

"I'm Detective Robert Heimbigner with the Seattle Police Department. I need your help. Brad tells me you grew up in eastern Washington. I'm from Yakima, myself. I understand you were in the navy."

"Yeah, for twelve years. I was a navy diver."

"Ever dive in the Persian Gulf? I hear the water there is very clear."

"Too many sharks for my taste. I dive for work, not thrills."

"I understand. I didn't come to talk about old military times, anyway. Do you know someone named Candice Mays?"

"I suspect you already know the answer to your question."

"You're right. I do. Just trying to break the ice. I

understand you gave her scuba diving lessons. When was that?"

"Last summer, July and August."

"How much did you see of her?"

"Just in class. About ninety minutes a week for eight weeks."

"When was the last time you saw her?"

"In August, at her check-out dive."

"What can you tell me about her?"

"Candice Mays is not her real name. I needed to know her real name for her C-card because it had to match her driver's license and also her passport if she dives internationally. Her name is Lisa Geld. She is twenty-one years old and from Memphis. I saw the information on her drivers' license. She said she is a college student somewhere in Florida. She was working as an exotic dancer for the summer in Seattle."

"A college student working as a stripper for the summer?"

"Yeah, don't they have strip clubs in Yakima or something? Lots of girls dancing in bars are college students earning their tuition. Good ones can turn a grand in a night without doing anything they shouldn't. Anyway, she planned to go back to Florida in mid-September for her senior year. I think the dive with Floyd was probably the last thing she did before leaving town. If you want to talk with her, I'd suggest you look in Florida."

The detective groaned. "Do you know how many colleges and universities there are in Florida?"

"A lot, I'll bet."

"Too many. Thanks for the information. Here's my card. If by any chance she didn't leave town and you happen to see her, give me a call."

"Sure, Detective Heimbigner. Good luck on your investigation."

Chapter 40

Brad asked Cathy to e-mail and text each person on the regular and per diem staff lists that attendance was mandatory at an unscheduled staff meeting for the following evening.

Five minutes before the meeting was to start, the department conference room was packed. Thirty-five of thirty-eight active staff were present. Precisely at 7:00 p.m., Brad came in from his office and stood at the front of the room.

"We are dealing with something serious and I need your help more than ever. We now believe several cases of carbon monoxide poisoning in town over the past few months were attempts by someone to injure or kill those poisoned. Some of the victims were treated by us and include a woman poisoned in her garage, two coffee bean roasters, a diver, and the widely publicized case of the Drinkwaters. Interestingly, the same kind of duct tape was used to seal the garage and the roasting ventilation system.

"While these individuals appear very diverse, the police have discovered they had one trait in common. None of them were ecologically minded.

"The Seattle Police believe this is the result of eco-terrorism. You may not know much about eco-terrorism, but organized groups with a common cause or belief usually perform it. It is typically directed against property. Buildings, factories, those sorts of things. However, there are examples where individuals and not groups have carried out acts of eco-terrorism. There have also been examples when people were targeted and not property. Do any of you know of groups in the Puget Sound area who might have extreme sophistication with regard to carbon monoxide and would go so far as to target non-green individuals?"

The hyperbaric staff team was quiet until Randy broke the silence. "Brad, if you think a bunch of us have formed an eco-terrorism group and are trying to kill people who aren't green, you're wrong. All of us love Seattle and the Pacific Northwest for its natural beauty and all of us know more than average about carbon monoxide poisoning. I have my ear to the ground around here and there is no organization like you describe among us."

Brad was surprised. "Randy, I did not mean to accuse any of you. You are great people and great employees. I just wanted to summarize the situation and see if it rang a bell for anyone, that's all. It was not my intent to offend you, and I apologize if I did."

Patti spoke up. "We should be under scrutiny because we do know a lot about carbon monoxide. However, the carbon monoxide knowledge these eco-terrorists apparently have can be acquired on the Internet. And half of it is on our own department's website in our department bibliography. I think because this team has such longevity in this department and has worked so many years together, we would know if a subgroup had gone off the deep end and become terrorists. I agree with Randy. That's ridiculous."

Brad nodded his head in agreement. "Again, I'm not accusing anyone in this room. I just want to know if you can think of anyone for whom this sounds the least bit familiar."

Claude spoke up. "After hearing you describe the entire issue, it makes me think I could know some guys similar to what you describe. I may have unwittingly given them the kind of information you are talking about. There are these two guys who come into my used dive gear shop on a Saturday about once a month. They have done so for about a year. They know I work here and are always asking me about what I do and whether there are any opportunities for them to get a job. We have gone out together to throw darts about three or four times. Every time we go, they want to hear about the most unusual cases we have treated. Since the routine patients are, quite frankly, boring, I have told them about several diving accidents and carbon monoxide poisoning cases. I am always careful to change the sex and age of the patients so there won't be a HIPPA violation. But I have told them about carbon monoxide poisoning while scuba diving, as well as carbon monoxide poisoning from charcoal and carbon monoxide diffusing through drywall. I thought I was just entertaining them, not telling them how to kill someone. In retrospect, I may have also told them about the ongoing investigation, I'm afraid. I bragged about the fact we were being asked to help the Seattle Police."

"Thank you for being open and honest. This information may help dramatically. Do you know their names, where they live, or how the police can find them?"

"I'm embarrassed to say I only know their first names, and they are confusing. Both are named William, so one goes by Willie and the other Bill. They've never bought anything in my shop, just looked around and asked me questions. I do know they work at Boeing and live down in Renton. They rent an apartment together and are always complaining their landlord never fixes anything."

"I think I know where to go next. Thanks for your help. And I want to reassure all of you I never suspected you for an instant. Have a good evening and thanks for coming in on short notice."

As the staff members found their ways out into the dark night with a steady drizzle coming down, Brad went to his office and called his college roommate. The detective agreed the two described by Claude should be investigated, and both men agreed their landlord sounded very much like Jerry Chinn. Bob expressed he did not feel like he got very far with Chinn during their prior meeting and asked if Brad would call him since they were better friends.

Brad agreed and told Bob he would give Jerry a call in the morning.

Chapter 41

B rad dialed Jerry Chinn's phone number, and Jerry answered on the first ring.

"Hi Jerry, this is Brad Franklin at Metropolitan Hospital. We went to college together."

"Oh, hi Brad. Sure, I remember you well. Pre-med, Mercer Island High School, decent pool player, always got the top grade in every class we shared."

"That's only because you weren't trying. Anyway, I called to follow-up on some things Bob Heimbigner came to talk with you about."

"When Bob visited me, he was interested in two things. How people get their hands on high-speed duct tape and what I know about suicide by charcoal in Asia. What's going on, anyway?"

"I need you to be confidential about this. The police are looking for what is likely a small group of people who are acting as eco-terrorists in the Seattle area. There is some reason to think two of them might be renting one of your apartments and working at Boeing."

"Really? What are their names?"

"We only know their first names and it is the same— William. One goes by Willie and one goes by Bill. How many apartment units do you own?"

"Now I need you to be confidential about this. About five hundred."

"Five hundred! What are you doing still working at Boeing?"

"That is top secret and I can't tell you. Anyway, I don't rent to two guys named William."

"How do you know? You have five hundred units. You are smart but you can't know all your renters off the top of your head."

"No, but I have a computer on my desk and can type while I talk on the phone. I just checked my renter database. No pairs of William or any combination of William, Willy, and Bill. Are these the guys who used the duct tape?"

"Yes, we think so. In one case, duct tape was used to seal a garage door. In another, it was used to tape a vent closed."

"Was the end of the tape cut with a knife or torn?"

"I don't know. Why?"

"DNA, my doctor friend, DNA. Remember the old double helix from biochemistry? Using duct tape on a job has become many a criminal's undoing. When they use it to tie up a hostage, they usually tear it. But duct tape can sometimes be difficult to tear. So, they may use their teeth to get it started. And DNA from saliva sticking to the duct tape may contain the information needed to identify them."

"How do you know this?"

"Well, I admit I first saw it on a television show. But it was so interesting I googled it and found out various crimes have been solved in this manner. And four-hundred-mile-per-hour metal duct tape is tough stuff, believe me. There is probably no one who can get the tear started with only their fingers. You have to use a knife or scissors or your teeth. So, if your duct tape is ragged on the end, you may have an answer to your search."

"Wow, thanks a million, Jerry. You've been a gold mine of information."

"Glad I was able to help. Talk to you down the road."

Chapter 42

Brad placed a call to Bob at lunchtime and told him what Jerry had said about duct tape.

"Doc, I know about duct tape DNA. DNA testing is very expensive. We did it on duct tape found at every crime scene for a while. Then word got out among the bad guys they should not tear it with their teeth because of the saliva contamination, and they got in the habit of tearing it with their hands. So we came up negative for DNA on test after test and wasted a lot of money. Now, I did not think about the fact 400-mile-per-hour duct tape is too tough to tear without getting it started by using your teeth or cutting it with a knife. I'll go down to the evidence lockers and see it this looks like it was torn or cut."

Just after he hung up, Patti walked into Brad's office and sat down. "I feel sick and think I need to go home. I have a headache, I feel nauseated, and I'm dizzy like I am going to fall down. I think I may have the flu."

"It's probably a different viral illness. You've had the flu shot just like every other employee at Metro, and you don't have any respiratory symptoms. It's also too early for influenza in Seattle. Influenza usually starts on the East Coast in the late autumn and spreads west, reaching our area around the end of January."

"You know, I don't really care about all that. I just know I feel like crap. I called Earl, and he is able to cover me."

"Go home, go to bed and get some rest. If you feel better in the morning, come on in. If not, stay home and we'll find coverage for you."

An hour after Patti left, Randy came up to Brad. "Boss, I don't want this to look like psychosomatic illness, but I think I have the same bug as Patti. It started just after I finished operating for the first treatment today and has gotten steadily worse. I've tried to keep busy helping the patients, but I feel terrible. At first, I just had a headache. Then came dizziness and the feeling I wasn't thinking clearly. Then nausea, and most recently, vomiting."

"Get out of here and go home before you give this to the rest of the staff and the patients. See you tomorrow."

As Randy walked slowly out the door, Brad noted he was beginning to get a headache. Like Randy, he knew medical professionals were susceptible to internalizing the symptoms of those sick around them, believing they have the same illness. But he really did have a bad headache. Since this was an administrative afternoon, he decided to go home and try to get some sleep. As he rode across downtown in an Uber vehicle, he wondered what they could all have been exposed to with such a similar incubation period. It reminded him of the teaching that if a family comes to the emergency room in the winter, all having gotten sick simultaneously, it's probably not influenza, but rather carbon monoxide poisoning.

Chapter 43

B rad got into work a half hour early the next morning, having awakened feeling well. He was pleased to see Patti and Randy were already in the department when he arrived, both feeling fine, also.

"Hey, you two. It appears you recovered overnight. That was the true twenty-four-hour bug, wasn't it?"

Carole was there as well, busy setting up the chamber for the six patients in the 8:30 a.m. routine two-hour treatment.

"I'm glad I wasn't here yesterday. Sounds like you guys caught something nasty but luckily it was short-lived. Patti, take it easy this morning. I'll check in on all the patients in the 8:30 treatment, get their vital signs, and herd them into the chamber."

Patti smiled in appreciation. "You may not be willing to try deep-fried turkey, Carole, but I like you anyway."

Carole hustled about, greeting each patient as they

arrived in the chamber room, escorting them to the assessment station for status review and blood pressure measurement, then accompanied each to the central "on deck circle" of comfortable lounge chairs where patients sat and chatted until it was time to enter the chamber at 8:25.

Brad had the day reserved for research and had no clinical duties. Just before lunch, Carole stood in the doorway of his office. "Brad, I think I caught it, too. I felt great when I got here, took care of all the patient duties prior to the treatment, then started feeling sick about one hour into the treatment. Headache, dizziness, nausea. Really lousy. After I went on oxygen breathing at the end of the treatment, I felt good again. But while checking out the patients and helping get them on their way, everything came back."

"Carole, if I didn't know better, I'd say it sounds like you have carbon monoxide poisoning. But we have monitors in the department and they all read zero parts per million on the console or Randy would not have compressed the chamber. How did you get to work? Did you drive your car? Could you have an exhaust leak?"

"Nope, I rode my bike."

"Will you humor me and let me check your carbon monoxide blood level with our pulse CO-oximeter? I just need to clip the probe on your fingertip for thirty seconds."

"Sure."

Carole sat down in his office chair and put her aching head between her hands while he retrieved the handheld instrument.

A few minutes later, Brad had measured Carole's level three times.

"I don't believe it. Your carbon monoxide level is 13 to 14%, telling us you were exposed to carbon monoxide sometime in the past several hours and probably explaining your symptoms. You got here feeling well, got sick after about two hours in the department, improved on oxygen, and then got sick again. I'm going to call the ED and tell them you are coming up for oxygen treatment of mild carbon monoxide poisoning. Stay in the ED until you feel well, then go home. I need to talk to Claude about carbon monoxide levels in the department."

Chapter 44

Before he had a chance to track down Claude, Cathy called from her desk. "Detective Bob on hold for you on line one."

Brad picked up the nearest department phone. "Hi, Bob. What have you got?"

"The duct tape from the garage and the tape from the coffee roasting facility were both saved in evidence bags. Guess what? Both samples were torn and not cut. And bingo! Both have DNA left from the person ripping them with his teeth. It is being run against criminal DNA databases as we speak. If those don't yield a match, we'll check databases of other people who have DNA samples collected, such as government employees with security clearance above a certain level, active duty or ex-military, and the like. If his, her, or their DNA is on file, we should know who it is within a week."

"Hopefully we'll get an answer from it. Jerry Chinn

will never let us forget it, but it will be worth it. In the meantime, something strange is going on right here in the hyperbaric department. Three of us went home sick yesterday and were well this morning after a night away from here. Now today, another nurse got similar symptoms after doing a lot of patient care and it turns out her blood carbon monoxide level is high. I'm not sure how to explain it."

"Doc, that one is yours to figure out. You know more about carbon monoxide than I do, although I've got you beat on catalytic converters."

"Call if you learn anything. Thanks for the DNA update."

Brad paged Claude to his office. "Claude, do you know where those portable industrial carbon monoxide monitors are? We need to walk around the department with them. I think people are getting exposed to carbon monoxide here."

"Yeah, I know where we stored them. I'll go get them. Do you think someone is trying to poison us now?"

"I don't want to jump to conclusions until we see if there is carbon monoxide somewhere in here. Bring the pulse CO-oximeter, too. Let's check some random levels, starting with our own."

Once the equipment was assembled, they measured each other's blood carbon monoxide level with the fingertip probe. Claude's was 5% and Brad's 8%.

"Since neither of us smoke, we are getting exposed to carbon monoxide somehow. I've spent the morning in my office. I have a carbon monoxide alarm with a digital readout plugged into the wall right there and the carbon monoxide level in here right now is zero parts per million. Where have you been?"

"Mostly in my shop. But there is no combustion going on in there and levels are zero, as well."

They walked across the department to the chamber area where Patti worked on the computer at the nurses' station. She recognized the device Claude carried, put out her finger, and he measured her level. In the meantime, Brad took an ambient reading.

"Now, here in the chamber area, levels in the air are zero and so is Patti's blood level. Patti, what have you done so far today?"

"Well, I've been here at the nursing station sitting on my butt for the most part. Carole took care of the patients by herself, and then got sick. But she was working right in this room, not thirty feet away. I have been working on policies on the computer and she was doing patient care. Can you get carbon monoxide from a patient?

"No, of course not. We need to figure this out. Tomorrow is Friday. We'll check everyone's carbon monoxide level when they get to work, then again every two hours during their shift. We'll also ask everyone to keep a log, recording where he or she is every thirty minutes. If there is a carbon monoxide source in here, we should be able to isolate it. Claude, recheck levels in every room a couple of times this afternoon. Then, I want you to coordinate the measurements tomorrow and collect each person's log sheet from them before they leave work."

"Okay. I sure don't understand how, but it looks like someone may be trying to poison the department staff with carbon monoxide."

"It's certainly possible."

Chapter 45

S itting in his office after the staff meeting, Claude had pretended to tinker with a broken chamber light in case anyone stopped by to talk to him. He thought about what else he might do to keep the focus of the investigation away from him. He also wanted to review events in his mind again to make sure there was not any reason to suspect him.

Poisoning Laurie Rodgers had been easy. He had attempted to kill her to make an example of people who are wasteful of energy resources by driving huge vehicles unnecessarily. He had hoped all those Hummer owners would get the message when the news came out she was found dead in her Escalade. He used his old trick of getting someone to write him a check to get her name and address. After going to her place early that Monday morning for reconnaissance, he knew her morning pattern. Then it was a simple matter to slip into her garage at 2:00 a.m., duct tape the garage door edges, and light a gallon-sized tin can of charcoal before slipping back out.

Poisoning Floyd had been just as easy. When he refilled Floyd's scuba tank, he set the end of the air intake hose near the exhaust port of his gasoline-powered compressor. In retrospect, he might have done things a little differently. He probably should have put carbon monoxide in both of their tanks so the event would appear more accidental. But Floyd had been his target, not Candy. Successfully poisoning both of them, however, would have obviated the potential for discovery if someone learned he actually had filled their tanks at his shop. He felt lucky Floyd was off in China. He was aware of the transient nature of exotic dancers from his naval tours and knew Candy would never be found, even if they were interested in locating her. She was probably dancing in Phoenix or Anchorage under another name. If investigators went looking for a college student named Lisa Geld in Florida, they would be looking for a very long time. He smiled at the thought.

Thanks to the education on carbon monoxide poisoning Brad had provided the staff, Claude remembered how he learned about the amount of carbon monoxide produced by roasting and grinding coffee beans. He had been irritated with Gregg from the start when he saw him wearing the T-shirt reading, "Spotted Owls Taste Like Fried Chicken." This was a slap in the face of environmentalists. Spotted Owls are a protected species on the Olympic Peninsula. They had stopped the logging industry there when it was discovered they were endangered, and their habitat was being destroyed. The loggers in Forks are not very environmentally conscious and certainly not fond of Spotted Owls. A common joke about their lack of environmental concern is the billboard in Forks reading, "Earth First. We'll log the other planets later."

When he found the warehouse on Airport Road near Boeing Field where the two jokers had set up their roasting operation to scam the public, a quick examination had revealed their exhaust hood was adequate but would be ineffective if obstructed. Again, he wished he had done it a little differently and not used the same duct tape for the job. He went to the Boeing surplus store about once a month to look for good buys on things they might need for the hyperbaric chamber. Aerospace tolerances are much higher than those in diving operations or hyperbaric facilities. He could get a better gauge there for a fraction of the price charged by the hyperbaric clearinghouse. Everyone who shops at Boeing Surplus picks up a roll of aviation duct tape. He kept a couple of rolls in his desk for use in the department and had been lazy when he used it twice.

Claude had poisoned the Drinkwaters on his day off. Conveniently, it was the week between sessions when he heard about Drinkwaters' involvement with Styrofoam on the news. Gasoline-powered electrical generators are notorious for their output of carbon monoxide, and the source of poisoning for many of the patients they treated in the hyperbaric chamber during power outages caused by storms. Unlike the old generators he had used in the navy, those manufactured now for use by homeowners were often so quiet you could barely hear them running. The Drinkwaters would have suspected something immediately if they had come home to a generator running in their living room.

Thanks to the recent revelation regarding carbon monoxide's ability to pass through gypsum wallboard with ease, he was able to set up a new generator in the upstairs storeroom adjacent to their bedroom and leave it running with the door closed. The carbon monoxide would diffuse through the wall and fill the bedroom. The generator would eventually run out of the half-gallon of gasoline he put in the tank, and when discovered, look like one the couple had purchased to have for emergencies.

Even though Washington State had a new law mandating the installation of carbon monoxide alarms in all residences, they were only immediately required in new construction. Until the Drinkwaters sold their home or had work done requiring a permit, they wouldn't be required to install one. And since Mr. Drinkwater had never been concerned about pollution, he would not go buy one electively.

The more Claude had pondered his actions to date, the more convinced he became no one could be the wiser despite a few minor errors. He had done well so far in striking a blow on behalf of the Earth. As it stood right now, everyone hopefully believed two Boeing employees living in Renton were committing the crimes, after receiving inadvertent education from Claude. If the department staff believed everything he had told them, the two suspects were aware the hyperbaric staff members were assisting with the investigation. If really true, Claude knew what the next move must be; the answer came to Claude like a lightning bolt.

Obviously, the suspects would try to poison the staff to prevent them from solving the crimes. The best way to support this new confabulation was for him to poison the hyperbaric department staff members with carbon monoxide. Although he had qualms about the idea, he considered how he could do it. These people were his friends. They may also be friends of the environment. Sure, they tossed an occasional empty aluminum soda can in the trash instead of the recycling bin. Sometimes they overrode the energy-saving motion sensor light controls he had installed throughout the facility to keep the lights from turning off when they worked at their desks. But those were not environmental issues worth killing someone over. And how could he poison the department staff without poisoning the patients? He did not want to hurt them, as they had done nothing to deserve it.

But carbon monoxide diffuses so rapidly through air, there would be no way to contain the gas in any one part of the department. The concentration would quickly equalize throughout the facility. Finally, many of the staff worked only per diem, coming in to be the inside attendant for a single routine treatment. It would take a matter of days for all of them to be present at one time in the department.

As he leaned back in his chair, his eyes scanned the contents of the shelves in his combination office and workshop. He noticed a gallon can of solvent on the top shelf and immediately knew the answer to all those questions.

Chapter 46

Methylene chloride, also known as dichloromethane, was a colorless liquid with a sweet aroma commonly used as a solvent and sometimes as a paint stripper. It was volatile, evaporating from liquid to gas phase rapidly. Because of this, most of the toxicity of methylene chloride was attributed to the effects of inhaling the compound. However, it could also be absorbed through the skin.

In addition to being a topical irritant to the eyes and respiratory tract, methylene chloride absorbed through the skin or lungs was metabolized to carbon monoxide, potentially leading to carbon monoxide poisoning. Common symptoms included confusion, dizziness, headache, nausea, weakness, and fatigue. More serious symptoms could include loss of consciousness, coma, and death. The degree of carbon monoxide poisoning from methylene chloride exposure depended on the amount of the compound absorbed.

Several years ago, alcohol-based hand sanitizers, such as the product Purell, became popular in hospitals and clinics as an alternative to hand washing. The products were extremely effective and easy to use. Alcohol rub sanitizers contained at least 70% alcohol and killed 99.9% of bacteria on hands within 30 seconds after application, when properly used. The user was instructed to apply enough gel to the palm of one hand to wet both hands completely, and then rub the product over all surfaces of the hands until they were dry. In reality, use of alcohol rub gels was much easier than hand washing with soap and water. Dispensers designed to release a pre-measured amount of alcohol gel were mounted on walls throughout medical centers. Health-care personnel were instructed to cleanse their hands before and after every patient encounter to prevent spread of pathogens. Use of the gels became such a habit for some in medicine, they "gelled" whenever they passed a dispenser. The average health-care worker used them thirty times per day.

Claude knew how frequently the hyperbaric staff took alcohol gel from the dispensers on the walls of the hyperbaric department to clean their hands, since it was his job to refill the dispensers when empty. He also knew about methylene chloride. Integrating those two pieces of information had given him the method he sought to cause carbon monoxide poisoning in his coworkers.

He was in the department until the early morning following the staff meeting. Claude collected all sixteen alcohol gel dispensers from the facility. He emptied each of them into a five-gallon plastic bucket. When all the gel was in the bucket, he measured its depth with a ruler. He then poured methylene chloride from the can in his workshop into the bucket until the depth of gel plus solvent was doubled. While alcohol gel was a little thick, he did not think the staff would notice a fifty-fifty dilution. Since the methylene chloride was clear and smelled sweet, its presence blended well with the fragranced gel.

Claude then filled the dispensers with the mix and replaced them. He knew each time someone used the gel to sanitize their hands, they would absorb a small amount of methylene chloride through their skin. For those who did more patient care, more would be absorbed because they would clean their hands before and after every patient contact. They would metabolize more into carbon monoxide and become more poisoned.

His planning had worked just as designed so far. He did not want to severely hurt or kill any of his friends. And they had cooperated perfectly. As each slowly got sick from the carbon monoxide poisoning, they had gone home and thereby stopped their exposure. Only if they had been forced to stay at work and continue to use the gel would they be at real risk. Claude predicted Brad would never force anyone feeling sick to stay at work and he hadn't. Claude was especially proud of the fact he had used the spiked gel on his own hands three times each morning. His own elevated carbon monoxide level had kept attention diverted from him.

Now he wondered how he was going to manage the situation the following day. Each person would have a log sheet in their possession, recording their location and blood carbon monoxide levels throughout the day. He knew if Brad was given the information along with negative ambient carbon monoxide levels throughout the department all day long, he was smart enough to figure out how they were getting poisoned.

Chapter 47

Both Claude and Brad arrived early. The physician had put together a data sheet for staff on duty to enter their name, time of arrival, and serial measurements of their blood carbon monoxide level and location within the department over their shift. He had a second data sheet for Claude, listing every room in the department, with lines for him to record ambient carbon monoxide levels in each place over the course of the day.

Brad said to Claude, "You'll be monitoring the situation on your own because I'm involved in a continuing medical education course in the hospital auditorium most of the day."

"That is just fine with me," thought Claude as he sighed inwardly with relief. He would have the opportunity to collect the data sheets and modify them. It should still work. He just needed everyone to believe someone outside the department was the source of poisoning.

Claude had topped off the alcohol gel dispensers with pure alcohol gel, thereby diluting the methylene chloride in them. His hope was blood carbon monoxide levels might rise a small amount, but no one would feel sick enough to bring it to Brad's attention and keep him around the department. In that way, the day might pass without interference in his plans.

The day proceeded smoothly, at least from Claude's standpoint. He recorded mildly elevated ambient air carbon monoxide levels scattered throughout the department over the course of the day, even though all were actually zero. When staff turned in their log sheets to him, Claude looked them over, then adjusted numbers of 3% or 4% to 13% or 14% by adding a digit. He had just finished his data "correction" when Brad returned at the end of the day. The patients and the rest of the staff were gone.

"How did things go today?" inquired Brad, when he found him in the engineer's office.

"From a process standpoint, they went fine. I got every measurement you wanted. From the standpoint of drawing any conclusions, I'm not sure. I was just reviewing the data and can't make heads or tails of it."

"That's okay, I'll review it over the weekend. Do you know if Detective Heimbigner called?"

"Not to my knowledge. Why?"

"Oh, I may not have mentioned it. You know the duct tape we have talked about at the staff meeting?"

"Yeah, sure. Why?"

"Well, we got a tip it might contain DNA from the person or people who poisoned all of these folks with carbon monoxide."

"How is that?" Claude asked, his voice cracking.

"It looks like the murderer used his teeth to tear it and left saliva DNA on the tape. The police are running the DNA profile against a large criminal database. If it doesn't yield an answer, they will run it against other federal DNA databases. We're hopeful to have an answer soon."

Reality hit Claude as if his scuba tanks had just run out of air. He knew his DNA had been collected by the navy in case he was killed in action and his remains needed to be identified.

As he watched Brad walk out the door, it felt like he could not breathe.

Chapter 48

B rad entered the chamber room Monday morning.
"Good morning Earl, nice to see you. Have you seen
Claude?"

"Hi Doc. No, I haven't. Can I help you?"

"I want to review the data sheets from our department carbon monoxide monitoring project Friday with
him. They make no sense. When he gets here, tell him I'd
like to speak with him. I'll be down in my office."

"Sure. Will do."

At 10:00 a.m., Cathy told Brad Detective Heimbigner
was at the department reception desk, asking to see him.
Claude had still not been seen. The physician walked out
of his office to greet his friend.

"Hi Bob. Any DNA news?"

"That's what I'm here about, Brad. Can we talk in
your office?"

"Sure. I can't wait to hear what you have to say."

"Don't speak too soon," replied the detective as he closed the door of Brad's office. "The DNA did not match any known criminal."

"Oh, no. We're still at first base."

"No, we're not. DNA from duct tape at both sites matched 100% to an individual in a federal government database. His name is Claude Fountaine. I'm here to arrest him on the charge of first-degree murder."

Brad was stunned, taking two steps back. "Claude? You've got to be kidding. I knew he was passionate about the environment, but I can't believe he would try to kill people."

"Do you know of any major life stresses Claude might have experienced that might have contributed?"

The issues poured through Brad's mind. "As a matter of fact, I do. Claude has told me about his background during the time we have spent together. He was born in Richland. His grandfather moved there during World War II to work on construction of the Hanford Site. Things ramped up with the arms race with the Soviet Union and by 1960, both his grandfather and father worked at Hanford. His grandfather died of lung cancer in his fifties, even though he never smoked. Claude's father died of thyroid cancer a couple years after he was born. Claude's mother passed away from leukemia while he was in community college."

"Did cancer run in his family?"

"Not until they moved to Hanford. Claude fully believes his grandfather and both parents died as the result of being downwinders."

The detective looks puzzled. "Okay Doc, you've got me. What are downwinders?"

"It's a term applied to people who get exposed to radiation from living near to or downwind from a nuclear facility. Probably due to that experience, Claude has always been a strong proponent of ecology and protection of the Earth. I have overheard him more than once telling other Department staff how people who don't respect the Earth may be hurting or killing others. But I still can't believe he would act out by killing people himself."

"This background information provides motive. I need to take him in. I wanted to talk to you first because I'd like to do this with as little commotion as possible. How would you like me to proceed?"

"He did not come to work today and did not call in. We called his cell phone and got voice mail."

"Great. Someone probably tipped him off and he's on the run. I need to find him. Where does he live?"

"Not far from here, on Capitol Hill. I'm afraid I may have been the one who tipped him off. I told him about the DNA evidence and the possibility these crimes might be solved soon. Let me go with you. I can show you where he lives and talk to him about surrendering to you if he is there. We don't need any more violence."

"You can come, but I'll be at your side all the way. I am not going to let him run."

"Okay. But just keep your trigger finger in check. Claude may possibly have poisoned some people, but he won't hurt me."

The two men rode in Bob's unmarked car to Claude's house.

Brad said, "That's Claude's pickup in the driveway with a gas can in the back. It looks like he's here."

"Okay. We can't give him the opportunity to get the drop on us. I know you said he won't hurt you, but remember he is military trained. It's likely he has weapons in there. We're not going up and ringing the doorbell. We'll enter through the garage and try to catch him off guard."

The detective used an iron bar to pop the door to the garage. The two men stepped in under the hand-painted sign reading, "Claude's Corner." The garage light was on.

Brad saw him first. Claude sat in an easy chair in the back, next to a hibachi grill filled with charcoal ash. There was no reason to check his pulse.

He was cherry red.

Acknowledgments

The author thanks the individuals who taught him about hyperbaric medicine, carbon monoxide poisoning, and diving medicine. Those "rock stars" know who they are, so all of their names will not be listed here. He further wishes to express special appreciation to his editor, Lorraine Fico-White, whose patience, attention to detail, and teaching enabled him to achieve his goal of making this book all it could be.

About the Author

Neil B. Hampson, MD

Dr. Hampson is currently Emeritus Medical Director of the Center for Hyperbaric Medicine at Virginia Mason Medical Center and Clinical Professor of Medicine in the University of Washington, both in Seattle.

He received his medical degree at the University of Washington and completed an internal medicine residency at the University of Iowa, then a pulmonary and critical care fellowship at Duke University. He spent one year as a faculty member in the Duke Department of Medicine, then moved to Virginia Mason in 1988. He served as Medical Director of the Center for Hyperbaric Medicine from 1989–2010. He is board-certified in internal medicine, pulmonary disease, critical care medicine and undersea and hyperbaric medicine.

He is past-president of the Undersea and Hyperbaric Medical Society, former Chairman of the UHMS Hyperbaric Oxygen Therapy Committee, and member of numerous UHMS committees and task forces.

Dr. Hampson's comprehensive work on the epidemiology and prevention of carbon monoxide poisoning has been extensively recognized. He has received the Paul Bert Award, Ray Award, Merrill Spencer Lifetime Achievement Award, and the Boerma Award, among others.

In 2015, he was awarded the Albert R. Behnke Award for lifetime achievement by the Undersea and Hyperbaric Medical Society. In his acceptance speech, he likened his individual teachers in hyperbaric medicine to various rock-n-roll stars instructing him to play rock music. He concluded, "While I may be old, I have seen all the cool bands."

Dr. Hampson's prior book, *Serial Chase: A True Story of the Lives and Deaths of a Doctor and a Deputy,* was true crime genre. It explored the tragic intersection of his grandfather's path with a serial killer in 1950.

Dr. Hampson met his wife, Diane, at the University of Washington when they were undergraduate physics lab partners. They currently divide their time between Puget Sound in the Pacific Northwest and the deserts of Arizona.